Samuel Greene Wheeler Benjamin

The World's Paradises

Or, sketches of life, scenery, and climate in noted sanitaria

Samuel Greene Wheeler Benjamin

The World's Paradises
Or, sketches of life, scenery, and climate in noted sanitaria

ISBN/EAN: 9783744793131

Printed in Europe, USA, Canada, Australia, Japan

Cover: Foto ©Andreas Hilbeck / pixelio.de

More available books at **www.hansebooks.com**

APPLETONS' NEW HANDY-VOLUME SERIES.

THE

WORLD'S PARADISES:

OR,

SKETCHES OF LIFE, SCENERY, AND CLIMATE IN NOTED SANITARIA.

BY

S. G. W BENJAMIN.

NEW YORK:
D. APPLETON AND COMPANY,
1880.

PREFACE.

WHEN the fall of Eve wrought the loss of paradise to man, the misfortune was not so irretrievable as appeared at first. So Milton thought, for, after composing "Paradise Lost," he seems to have changed his opinion on the subject, and sang of "Paradise Regained." If the race no longer reposes in the enchanted bowers of Eden, they find instead many Edens scattered over this varied and beautiful world, which, like the fair progeny of a peerless mother, suggest in their own lineaments the opulence of the maternal charms.

The simple fact that the word *paradise* comes from the Sanskrit, which seems to be as nearly allied as any tongue to that of our primitive ancestors, serves as an additional testimony to the elemental value of that language;

for we owe to it the word, and therefore inferentially the idea, which expresses the two most important periods in the existence of the human race. *Paradeso* is the Sanskrit term from which is derived our word paradise, that with various modifications is used wherever Scripture is known and men of the Indo-European races live and die. In paradise the human race began to be, and in paradise it will reach the final stage of its development. However men may disagree in the exact definition of this word and these periods of existence, they are commonly agreed in the general truths expressed by the word paradise.

How the term came to be used in this sense we find not a difficult matter to settle. The Greeks, borrowing the idea from the Persians, called a large park, intended for pleasure and the chase, a *paradise*. Those who are familiar with Xenophon will often find the word so used in his writings. The secondary meaning we apply to the word, as a spot of extraordinary attractions and fitted for ease, pleasure, and health, is really a blending of the Greek and the

Scriptural ideas. It suggests at once the golden age of our ancestors, when innocence and happiness are supposed to have dwelt hand-in-hand in a greenwood where sorrow, pain, or sin entered not, and a world to which we may retreat at last from the rugged conflict of life in a sphere which all agree to consider corrupt and unsatisfying. The best that men remember or that they hope for is thus included in the word paradise.

It is therefore only natural that man should often turn with longing and rapture to such delicious retreats as the world offers here and there, and, calmed by the seductive influences of a lovely scenery and a genial climate, half forget the stern realities of existence, and imagine himself actually in an elysium whose charms seem to him perpetual.

There have been in all ages certain magical spots which nature has endowed with a special enchantment—places sung by the poets and immortalized by perennial fame in the heart of the nations. There the weary have sought and often found rest, and those oppressed with dis-

ease of the body or the soul have felt their
languors pass away.

It is evident that an earthly paradise, in
order that it may be beneficial as well as attractive, should combine with beauty of scenery
restorative climatic conditions that make it salubrious to the invalid as well as agreeable to the
pleasure-seeker; or it should, at least, be so far
free from noxious characteristics as to render it
reasonably safe from malaria or epidemics. It
is because of the absence of such sanitary qualifications that many of the most seductive retreats of the tropics can not be wisely visited,
for too often they allure to destroy; the fatal
miasma lurks in their loveliest nooks, as the
sumptuous Venetian rings of old sometimes
pierced and insidiously instilled a poisonous
dew into the fingers they adorned.

It is in the north temperate zone that we
find most of those famed spots to which the
artist and the poet, the voluptuary and the invalid, have resorted for ages, and found solace
alike for body and soul. And two vast adjoining regions, dependent mainly on air and water

currents for their attractions, commend themselves especially to our attention in this connection. These are the basin of the Mediterranean and the North Atlantic between the latitudes of London and Havana.

Some of these favored spots may be recommended as sanitariums during the whole year; others only during certain seasons. But he must be capricious indeed in temperament, or completely exhausted in physique, who can not among them all find some resort that will suit his particular needs.

CONTENTS.

WORLD'S PARADISES.

DAMASCUS.

UNTIL modern travel and increasing means of communication added to our knowledge of different parts of the globe, and enabled us to visit them, it was natural that the gorgeous East should be the center of the world's paradises. Who has not heard of the vale of Cashmere, lying green in the lap of the mountains, and sheltered from the rude blasts and ruder men of the outer world?

There, too, is Bagdad by the tawny flood of the Tigris, shaded by clusters of palms, and glittering with gilded domes and minarets, first called the City of Peace, and far famed for its luxury and splendor in the days of Haroun-al-Raschid. Inclosing palaces and fountains within encircling battlements, and overarching groves that shielded it from the heat of the noonday sun, it well deserved to be ranked among the paradises of the East.

But Damascus has for thousands of years been the most famous spot on the globe for the glory of its attractions. The oldest of the world's cities now existing, and the oldest in the universe, per-haps—the burden of the proof is with those who deny it—lapped on a verdurous plain by the side of murmuring streams, wars have swept over it in vain, for it still remains Damascus the peer-less. The secret of its loveliness is, however, very simple, if one cares to analyze it. In the steady, protracted heat of that climate, not so much excessive as continuous, nothing is more grateful than shade and running water, with abundance of flowers to perfume the air, and fruits for idle hours. All these conditions are found admirably combined at Damascus. The houses are built in the form of a hollow square around a court paved with marble, in the midst of which is a fountain surrounded by clambering vines, roses, and jasmines, and vaulted over by the dense foliage of mulberry, orange, fig, and linden trees, and pomegranates studded with scar-let buds. Stepping from the narrow, crooked, dusky street, gloomed by meeting eaves, one sud-denly finds himself in a paradise of ease, whose quiet and repose are admirably adapted to soothe the nerves of the weary.

Another cause of the celebrity of Damascus

has doubtless been the manner by which it is approached. After a wearisome and exhausting journey over the desert of Mesopotamia, or the far more arid sands that lie between Egypt and Palestine, the traveler sees before him, on a vast plain, a long line intensely dark and green, resembling the shadow of a heavy cloud brooding over the landscape. As he approaches it the dark mass resolves itself into the dense foliage of palm, mulberry, fig, orange, linden, and chenar trees, lading the swooning air with perfume and filling the city with grateful shade.

Throwing himself on the ample divan by the side of air-cooling fountains, almost overpowered by the fragrance of roses, and through the bubbling narghilé inhaling the delicate narcotic of Iran, the traveler naturally imagines himself in the heavens of Mohammed. " In the name of God the most merciful ! " he ejaculates with fervor as he quaffs the sherbet in a gilded goblet, or presses his teeth in the honeyed pulp of the purple grapes of Lebanon, reclining on the embroidered cushions of the ample divans which surround the *salaamlik* or reception-saloon, that bids him welcome to ease and luxury fit for the pleasance of kings.

There are antiquities in Damascus ; there is even a street there yet which St. Paul is said to have trod—the street called Strait. "Peace ! let the dead past bury its dead," is again the thought of the true believer and native Damascene. "The past is past, and as for the hereafter, God is great! Are not the houris of to-day better than the possible ones of the future? Are not Abana and Pharpar, lined with flowers, still the rivers of Damascus? Is not the present in our grasp, O son of my uncle? Hath paradise aught more graceful than the interweaving lines of yonder smoke, eerily soaring from my chibouque toward the infinite? Why measure bliss or undertake to compare it? Is not rapture rapture, wherever, whenever, however enjoyed? I am in Damascus; 'tis enough.—Achmet, another pipe!"

And when the trill of the nightingale floats on the air of twilight, and the city swoons in the deep orange hues of the fading day, and the cypress and the palm, like motionless sentinels, stand dark against the sky tipped with stars, and the cry of the muezzin lingers and dies in long cadences over the battlements and far off over the plain, then Damascus wakes, and the revelry and the din of wassail begin. At mid-day she slept; at midnight the flash of her torches reveals the gleam of lambent and passionate eyes behind the gilded lattice or by the silver spouting fountains of marble.

Fired by draughts of anisette, the *almeh* in gauze-like garb shows the voluptuous lines of her dazzling form in the mystic undulations of the Oriental dance, while murmurs of applause are heard from her spectators as she alternately beats the tambourine with energy and springs into the air as if winged, or seems to float away in the soft languors of overpowering rapture.

One such evening I saw the Karaguez, or Punch and Judy of the East. Satire, the broadest and keenest, pointed the shafts of its mirth, and the scene, by the torches of the summer evening, was one of extraordinary picturesqueness. The sallies of wit, the chattering and pantomime of the puppets, the eager faces of the turbaned groups, exhibiting anything but Oriental stolidity, formed a spectacle that was intensely vivid in its characterization. Of the music on such occasions it is impossible to speak from the scientific point of view of the European composer; for its principles are of the rudest; the instruments are chiefly primitive guitars, tambourines, kettle-drums, and castanets; and whether vocal or instrumental, the tunes, if they can be so called, consist of a succession of quick, sharp notes, rising rapidly to a high key, and dying away in lingering cadences that exasperate the blood to the last degree. I can not say that I ever heard any musical harmony in the East worth the mentioning, but I have never listened to any sounds that so excited the senses as Oriental music; and I can easily understand the effect it produces on the warm-blooded children of the sun.

While meriting its celebrity because of the richness of its charms, Damascus in the spring-time can also be considered a valuable resort for those who are in need of absolute rest, and can resign themselves without reserve to the soothing influences of its pleasant air and sumptuous gardens and halls. If invalids would but abandon all thought or effort beyond the simple duty of enjoying the beautiful around them and breathing the pure air of a temperate and steady climate, they might often throw physic to the dogs, and reduce the emoluments of the faculty. Pure air, even and moderate temperature, rest—these are the three prime remedies of nature, whose supreme importance is becoming better understood every year in the treatment of chronic maladies.

BRUSA.

ANOTHER famed Eden and health resort of the East lies at the foot of Mount Olympus. It is Brusa, in Bithynia, the first capital of the Turkish Empire, but founded long before Christ by Prusias, and the scene of the last days of that greatest soldier of the ages, Hannibal of Carthage.

After being in the saddle from three in the afternoon, we brought up within the walls of the old city about midnight. All was silent except the dashing of water down the steep streets from the mountains, or the yelping of vagrant curs. The hostel where we sought a meal and a couch was on a narrow, sloping street. The landlord was a fat Teuton. The clatter of the horses did not arouse him. Only after pounding long and loud at the iron-bound gate, that awoke all the echoes of the sleeping town, did we at last succeed in bringing him, leaden-eyed, to the door, with a guttering candle.

But his hospitality soon became apparent, and he led us up to a noble hall, where he bade us welcome, while he bestirred himself to prepare a sumptuous meal.

At two in the morning we discussed the dinner, elegantly served and prepared, with the various delicacies for which the Turkish *cuisine* is famous; for our host, although a German, employed a native cook. Entremets, *piláff*, pastry, and what not, led us by easy gradation and genial converse to the final coffee and pipes; and then to slumber, in apartments once occupied by an Osmanli of rank; for the hotel was located in what had once been a *konák*, or residence of wealth.

At morning, unexpectant of the scene that unfolded itself, I flung open the jalousies, and, leaning on the window-sill, looked down upon one of the world's paradises. Fame has not exaggerated the opulence of its charms. The moss-green tiles of the city's peaked roofs, the domes, the mina-

2

rets, the gardens, lay spread below, embosomed
in a sea of verdure, bounded in the distance by
the blue waters of the Marmora.

Across a plain of wonderful beauty, skirted by
the sea, rises the enormous range of the Bithyn-
ian Olympus, ten thousand feet high. Its rugged
ridge is clad in eternal snows. Near the base of
this mountain, and partly on an outlying spur that
reaches out on the plain like the resting foot of a
couchant lion, lies the paradise of the Grand Turk,
for situation and beauty scarcely surpassed by any
city of the East.

The melting snows of Olympus form many
streams, which rush foaming through the streets
of the ancient city with perpetual music, blending
with the cooing of the turtle-doves that haunt the
cypress shade in the marble courtyards of the
mosques, and the nightingales that warble by the
sequestered mausoleums of the founders of a once
mighty empire.

During several reigns, the Sultans of Turkey
held their court at Brusa. Their palace and citadel were on the brow of the steep hill which overlooks the lower town, and is still the site of several interesting half-ruined structures, including
the mosque and tomb of the founder of the empire.
Centuries after his death one of his descendants
again made this his capital, and reigned at Brusa
for seventeen days. Zizim, the brother of Bayazid II., destined to die for no other crime than

because he was younger brother of the Sultan—a capital fault in the Ottoman dynasty until within forty years—revolted, and with a large army held sway at Brusa. Twice defeated, however, by treachery, on the plains below, he fled, raised another army, and brought the Sultan to the verge of destruction by his energy and ability. Finally forced to fly a second time, he sought refuge with the Knights of Rhodes, who broke their faith, and for many years kept him immured in a castle in Dauphiny. There he bewailed his family, whom he never saw again, composed some of the noblest lyrics in the Turkish language, which are still highly prized by Orientalists, and stole a passing solace in the sympathetic love of the daughter of the castellan of Sassenage. Their descendants are still found in the south of France.

Taken at last from the dungeon for diplomatic purposes, Zizim saw a powerful coalition of European princes formed to set him on the throne of Constantinople. At that critical moment the treasures of Bayazid availed to purchase the coöperation of Borgia, and on his way to empire again the unfortunate prince was poisoned by the agents of the Pope. His remains were transported to Turkey and buried in the city where for seventeen days he reigned with pomp and majesty, gazing with eagle eye over the paradise of Brusa. The royal annals of modern times offer us few histories more romantic than the career of Zizim.

Brusa is celebrated for its manufactories of silk stuffs, which hardly yield to any others in the East, and also, in addition to its perennial charms, claims attention as a sanitarium on account of its thermal springs that issue at a boiling heat from the mountain-side. The water is impregnated with sulphur and other minerals especially suited to rheumatic and cutaneous diseases, and is utilized by being caught in sanitary baths, arranged after the Turkish style.

Nothing in the external aspect of the building I visited suggested that it was constructed over steaming geysers. Entering a long, spacious hall paved with marble and surrounded by amply cushioned couches, where bathers were reclining after the bath, sleeping, or smoking the aromatic narghilé, it was with surprise that I learned, on passing into the vestibule hazy with dense volumes of steam, that the vapor was not produced by artificial heat. Treading over the hot floor with clogs on my feet, I passed, in a state bordering on complete evaporation, into the main bathroom, an immense hall, barely lighted by bull's-eyes in the vaulted ceiling, and seemingly quivering with the gray fog of the geysers. The bathers, reclining here and there on the marble, were singing to themselves, but their voices seemed far off and like echoes in a dream.

The *tellâk*, or bathing attendant, led me to the farther side of the hall, and there the rough rock of the mountain was seen projecting into the apartment, and the steaming water bursting forth in a highly choleric condition. But so parboiled had I become by this time, that when he placed my back against one of these hot streams gushing out like molten lava, the sensation was actually agreeable. The "subsequent proceedings" are best described by the word time. To reënter the reception-hall, to recline on its couches, to drink the fragrant berry of Araby, to smoke, to sleep, to dream—all this takes time, and without it half the advantages of the Oriental bath are wasted. The voluptuous fascinations of opium are not more delicious than the lethean and life-restoring repose that one may enjoy if he so wills after the otherwise enervating delights of the Turkish bath.

I left the bath as the sun was going down behind the purple crags of Olympus; and buoyed up by the most exquisite sensations, as if I were floating on the atmosphere rather than treading the ground, as I gazed entranced over the magnificent landscape, it seemed indeed one of the loveliest paradises yet seen by the eye of man.

THE BOSPORUS.

It is but a short night's sail from Modania, the port of Brusa, across the Sea of Marmora to the ivied walls of Constantinople, and its

gilded domes and minarets, rising in clustered
glory, tier above tier, along the steep shores of
the Golden Horn, surrounded by myriads of gayly colored dwellings, and skirted by the waters
crowded with picturesque shipping, and flowing
at the feet of the imperial city like molten turquoise. Eastward and northward spread the
waves of the Marmora and the Bosporus, encircled by shores lined with palaces and groves.
Lisbon and Naples and Rio Janeiro pale compared with a scene in which nature and man have
combined to produce the utmost degree of splendor of which we yet have any knowledge. The
imagination is dazed, the senses are almost
stunned, by the external magnificence of Stamboul. There may be other places where nature
has been as bountiful, other cities where the
monuments are as resplendent, although we question it; but there is none that presents both of
these elements so harmoniously united.

The shores around the port of the Golden Horn
rise so regularly and abruptly as to give the many-
colored houses which line them in myriads, tier
above tier, the appearance of gayly decked spectators in a vast amphitheatre. The gilded and
historic dome of Santa Sophia, accompanied by
the cupolas of numerous mosques, the glittering
crescents of a crowd of minarets, and the blood-
red banners of a multitude of gayly carved and
painted ships ranged along the shore, close by the

crumbling battlements and massive gateways and towers of the double walls erected by Genoese and Byzantine, add a matchless splendor to a scene which can be scarcely heightened when the setting sun fires dome and spire, veils the waters and palaces with a golden mist, and suffuses the ravines with purple gloom. But this wonderful spectacle, complete in itself, a dream to be inclosed within the memory like a pearl without a flaw, is but the vestibule to a succession of scenes which entrance the fancy and shape the character of him who has once offered incense at the shrine of the genius of this enchanted land.

From the Sea of Marmora we enter the Golden Horn ; but where the two unite begins the Bosporus, a winding strait flowing sixteen miles to the Black Sea. This is one of those places which from the earliest periods have attracted the attention of mankind ; and the legends that cluster about it carry us back into the remotest past. One advantage which the Bosporus enjoys above its rivals, the Rhine and the Hudson, is its brevity. They are too extended for full appreciation except by a regular journey ; but it is obvious that within sixteen miles the resident can in a morning's row behold the matchless splendors of the Thracian strait one by one unfold themselves, without the necessity of shooting by so rapidly as to be unable to contemplate them with satisfaction.

The Bosporus is inclosed by steep hills, which

decline so rapidly to the water that the largest ships can anywhere lie alongside the land. These hills are indented with gorges and valleys, which occur generally where the land retires and forms the most beautiful and inviting coves. A continuous series of summer-houses and palaces lines the shores, the kiosks often actually overhanging the water, and flanked by the most delicious gardens and terraces, planted with every variety of favorite flowers and shrubs. The valleys and ravines, on the other hand, are clustered with villages, whose tiled and moss-green roofs steeply rise one above the other in picturesque confusion up the precipitous sides of the hills. Through the center of the village rushes a brawling stream, hastening to meet the waters of the Bosporus. There, where the ravine widens, spreads a mall overarched by magnificent groups of stately chenars and stone-pines, murmuring the music of the sea. There the children play. There the sleepy sentinel paces the live-long day before the crumbling guard-house. There the *caffegee* prepares his coffee and pipes, and bears them with Oriental courtesy to the gray-bearded elders of the hamlet, who daily meet there to exchange the gossip of the neighborhood, to gaze on the idle ships floating by, and to muse over the beauty of the landscape, robed in the purple splendors of an Oriental sunset. When the shades of evening have closed in on this peaceful scene, the tinkle of the lover's guitar floats by the gliding waters, which reflect the quivering lights of fleets and towns ; and when all are at last hushed in repose, the nightingale wakes and flings her passionate warblings over the serene stillness of the Bosporus.

It is not strange that the Bosporus should have been for all ages a place of romance and story, of scenes of love too often ending in tragedy. If I were to narrate all the tales I have heard connected with the Bosporus simply during the last few years, it would be to compose a volume longer than the " Arabian Nights." An amusing escapade occurs to me in this connection, that was, however, less entertaining to the actors who took part in it. A young Englishman of wealth, while passing a few hours of ease at one of the many attractive spots along the shores of the Bosporus, saw among a group of Armenian girls one who suddenly attracted his attention in a manner unusual even to his susceptible heart.

She also, at the same instant, was impressed by the appearance of this tall, slender, aristocratic foreigner. He ordered his attendant to follow the ladies unperceived, and ascertain who they were and where they dwelt. The wily Greek soon obtained the desired information by opening an acquaintance with their servant. To make a long story short, a lively correspondence was soon started between the lovers—for lovers they were at first sight. The East may seem slow, dull, languid, but its passions are volcanic, and it takes but a spark to develop them into an ungovernable violence. The correspondence was of course carried on through third parties, and at first was in the suggestive language of flowers ; but it ended in a serious proposal that the young lady should fly across the seas with her lover. Already betrothed to one of her own countrymen, the fair Armenian well knew that she could never win the consent of her family to marry the proud young Englishman and exile herself from them in foreign lands.

＊ The idea of marrying her betrothed had now become intolerable, and she consented to elope. Her sister, who had to be taken into the secret, and who was neither young nor handsome, entered heartily into the arrangements. She encouraged her sister's failing resolution, and without her assistance the affair might have ended in smoke.

The destined night arrived, and the Englishman, burning with ardor, also arrived under the window of his beloved. He was accompanied by a faithful attendant and fleet horses champing to bear the lovers away to the sea. The sisters also were at the casement, and a ladder was lowered, but the lady hesitated to descend. Perhaps she then realized what it was to incur the wrath of her family, to break the heart of her betrothed, and to throw herself into the arms of a stranger.

Perhaps she also feared that she might fall from the rope ladder ; the night was dark, and an accident was more than possible.

Whatever the reason, the lady hesitated at this critical moment. Every instant was precious, discovery would be fatal, and yet the lady hesitated. It was in vain that her sister urged and expostulated with her.

"Well," said the older sister, "he shall not be disappointed, and if you will not go, I shall."

Thus saying, she resolutely stepped on the ladder, and in a moment was in the lover's arms. The night was dark, as was before observed, and as he lifted her on the horse he supposed she was the younger sister. They were soon at the water's side ; a boat was waiting, and they hurried on board the ship that was to bear them to other lands.

It was not until day broke that the Englishman discovered the deception that had been practiced upon him. But he was a man and a hero. When they reached the destined port he married the lady ; and although he never quite recovered the shock of the disappointment, he found solace in the pursuits of literature, and achieved a permanent position as an historical author.

It is difficult, where everything is so choice and beautiful, to select any particular scenes as surpassing the rest. Nevertheless, there are certain parts of the Bosporus which seem more espe-

cially to combine the grandeur and beauty of this
matchless strait.   One of these is where the shores
approach most nearly to each other, at the spot
where Darius carried his army across and Mohammed II. made his first lodgment in Europe.
The two deep coves of Bebek and Kandillee, being opposite to each other, present the appearance
of a lake protected on the northern side by the
grim white towers of Roumelee Hissar, and on the
southern bank by the yellow ivied walls of Ana-
dolee Hissar, whose battlements serve as windows
to the quaint houses that were built there after the
garrison was withdrawn and the castle was left to
slow decay.

By the foot of this old ruin glides the tranquil flood called the Heavenly Waters, a stream
that issues from the mountains of Asia Minor ;
as it approaches the Bosporus it flows through
broad meadow-lands carpeted with a profusion of
wild flowers.   Near the margin stands a marble
summer-house of the Sultan, glittering with gilded
lattices and surmounted by the flashing crescent
and star.   Here on festal days flock the gayly ap-
pareled folk of the neighboring villages, while on
the banks some primitive workers in clay, with
the simple potter's wheel of ancient times, turn
out earthenware vessels from age to age, illus-
trating the great fact that through all the muta-
tions of time the race begins and ends with the
sod of the valley.

From this magical spot we direct the gayly clad boatman of our swift caïque to row us past castle and town to the Bay of Buyukdéré.* The lines of the landscape at Buyukdéré take a wider sweep. Dominating this lake-like expanse of waters, the mighty height called the Giant's Grave rises opposite Buyukdéré.

In the valley adjoining the village yet soars the vast plane-tree, with a trunk one hundred and twenty feet in circumference, under whose shade Godfrey de Bouillon and his army encamped. Sheltered by lofty hills from the northern winds, this is perhaps the choicest spot along the Bosporus for invalids. There are no finer summer-houses, no sites more superb, no prospects more magnificent, than one sees as he saunters from this spot along the pier, until he is opposite to the crumbling castle which stands on the site, and is built of the stones of the old temple of Jupiter Urius.

This edifice was built at least twelve hundred years before Christ, and crowns the summit of a lofty hill on the left side of the Bosporus.

---

* The caique is to the Bosporus what the gondola is to Venice. Less funereal in appearance, fleet and graceful, furnished with scarlet cushions and decorated with gilded carvings, it is propelled by oarsmen in flowing white sleeves and red caps. The bosom is left bare, and their brown arms are sinewed with steel. Reclining in a caïque on a May morning, one achieves the poetry of motion.

From here we gaze on the winding waters of the strait, terminating with the spires of Stamboul, and over the broad, receding line of the blue Euxine and the northern mouth of the Bosporus. Jason and his companions, going after the Golden Fleece, stood there. Since that day Persian, Greek, Roman, Byzantine, Crusader, Islamite, and Frank have stood there in turn as conquerors, and have gazed and wondered ; for earth scarcely holds a prospect more beautiful, more alluring, more enchanting.

It is the crowning glory of this region that the climate is not only seductive, but salubrious, except from December to February inclusive, when the days are sometimes harsh and rude. The situation of the Bosporus, between the Black Sea on the north and the Marmora on the south, has much to do with tempering the air and rendering it equable. The rigors of winter are moderated and shortened by the warmth of the southern zephyrs, while the raging heats of summer are cooled by the breezes wafted down from the Euxine. Thus extremes are rare, and after the arrival of March the days are few when the invalid finds the climate morose and intolerable.

SMYRNA.

"SOUTHWARD, for ever southward," let our bark speed thence ; for other scenes invite, scarcely less attractive than these, adding by variety to the charm of life.

Who has not eaten the figs and raisins of Smyrna, the "ornament of Asia," the "crown of Ionia"? Situated at the head of a broad, beautiful bay, environed with perennial gardens, girt with a diadem of lovely villages, fragrant with the odorous airs that lade the serene Ægean skies, dowered with a wealth of historic associations, still dispensing fruits with a liberal hand, watched by the old Roman citadel, the grim battlements of the knights of St. John still reflected in the waters of her port, the city of the Moslem, the Greek, and the Frank is a living poem, but a poem of Byron's, fervid with the romance, the passions, and the crimes of the East. He who has sojourned there a fortnight dreams of her in his subsequent wanderings ; and he who has happily dwelt there for years longs for her in other lands, and sighs that destiny separates him from the vineyards and olive-groves, the villas and ruins, the Caravan Bridge and the bazaars, the delicious breezes and star-eyed maidens of Smyrna. So cordially does she welcome the child of the West to her bosom, that no city of the Levant

can boast so large a proportion of foreign residents.   So considerable, in fact, is the Christian
population, that the Turks call the place Giaour
Ismir—infidel Smyrna.

There are antiquities in and around the city of
Smyrna of sufficient interest, chief among them
the walls and towers of the castle crowning the
brow of Mount Pagus, immediately in the rear of
the Turkish quarter, which are well worth visiting.   From the old ramparts a magnificent view
is obtained over the city below, the gulf stretching far away, encircled with mountains, and the
gardens and villages whose verdure gives life to
the prospect.   Near by are the remains of the ancient Stadium, where Polycarp was burned, and
where many other Christians steadfastly endured
the onset of wild beasts and the horrors of the
stake.

In the days when the Janizaries acted as a
standing threat against the life of any Christian,
and foreigners lived in Turkey almost as secluded
as they did until recently in China or Japan, the
English, French, or Italian merchants had their
magazines and dwellings built on narrow, high-
walled courts, extending from Frank Street to the
Marino or Water Street, each end of the court
being protected by massive iron-studded gates, that
are closed at nightfall : every court has also one
or more porters, who carry the merchant's goods
by day and mount guard for him at night.   They

are magnificent fellows, rarely under six feet in
height, and proportionably sturdy. They are more
nearly the descendants of the original Ottoman
stock than any of the subjects of the Sultan.
These porters come from Ushâk and Aidin ; the
former is the place where the famous Turkish carpets are woven by the hands of women into such
gorgeous and enduring patterns. When a lad is
born at Ushâk his relatives ejaculate, " May he
become a good Smyrna *hâmal!* " On reaching
manhood he goes thither to live until he has
amassed sufficient to enable him to return and
pass the remainder of his days under the patri- .
monial fig-tree. The weight these porters carry
on their backs is something enormous.

The magazines on these courts are usually one
story in height, and on part of the roof, which is
flat, the house is built, the remainder of the roof
serving as a sort of hanging garden on which to
keep flowers, to promenade, or to sit at evening
and watch the sun set over the sea, to smoke,
take coffee, and chat. These terraces are also
admirable positions for kite-flying, which is conducted in Smyrna on a scale unknown in most
parts of the world.

The kite season begins toward the last of February, and continues until May. A hundred kites
may sometimes be counted in the air at once ; and
what gives to the pursuit a singular interest is the
circumstance that the Smyrniote manœuvres his

3

kite as he would a boat or a horse, and these
aërial toys may often be seen skirmishing and
fighting in this way for hours. Skill and practice are requisite in the construction and manage-
ment of the kite for this airy warfare, which is
not confined to boys, but is also engaged in by
older persons, and thus forms a diversion far
more exciting than the insipid sport followed in
America.

I once lived in a haunted house in one of those
dark courts. It had not been occupied for several
years, owing to its uncanny reputation. The rooms
were built on one side of a hall one hundred and
forty feet long, lighted on the opposite side by a
row of small windows near the lofty ceiling, like
port-holes in a frigate. Narrow passages led off
into dark attics and stairways. But we were unmolested by anything more spectral than rats.

During the fig season some of these courts are
the scene of a spectacle that is interesting to such
as consider dried figs one of the indispensable
luxuries of Thanksgiving and Christmas. Large
quantities of the fresh fruit are brought into
Smyrna on the backs of camels, which march
solemnly through the narrow streets in long pro-
cessions, to the monotonous beat of a bell fastened
to the pack-saddle of the leading camel. In front
of each string of camels trudges a meek, Carmelite-
looking little donkey, across whose back strides
the camel-driver, wearing a huge turban on his

head and an enormous sheepskin cloak on his shoulders, beating the leathern sides of the imperturbable beast with his long legs in unison with the clang of the camel-bell. Thus the slow train moves into the court of the foreign merchant or shipper, and the camels, after much grumbling on their part, are made to kneel down and deposit their cargoes. Since the railroads to Aidin and Kasaba have been opened, the "ships of the desert" have had some of the wind taken out of their sails, but it will be a long while yet before they are entirely superseded.

The figs, which have either green or purple skins, and are pulpy and pear-shaped when they are fresh, are steeped in a solution of salt and water, and collected in heaps on mats laid over the pavement of the court. Around these mats gather women from the country, sitting on the ground, barefooted, and working over the figs with their fingers, each fig being thus manipulated and prepared for packing. These women are accompanied by their children, who nurse while the mother is at work, or sport around, also barefooted, and greatly in need of a good washing, and occasionally while scuffling they chase each other over the piles of figs. It is a very amusing sight to those who do not intend to eat any of the figs.

After this kneading process the fruit is packed in drums, the smaller ones at the bottom, a layer of superior figs and a few olive leaves being laid

at the top to take the eye of the purchaser. Fruit
in Smyrna does *not* " grow bigger downward in
the box." A few drums are filled entirely with
the best quality of figs for those who choose
to pay for them. The drums are carried to the
quay and taken out to the ships in lighters. The
manner of getting them on board is unique. A
plank is swung over the ship's side half way between the lighter and the gunwale, and a man is
stationed on it. There are also two men in the
lighter alongside. One of them picks up a drum
and tosses it to the other, and he throws it to the
man on the plank, and he in turn to a man at the
bulwarks, who flings it to another standing at the
hatchway, who drops it into the hands of a stevedore in the hold, who gives it a final toss to the
stevedore who stows it in its place. The effect is
very odd, as the process goes on hour after hour
with the regularity of a piece of machinery.

When a house is roofed in the East the tiles
are sent up to the eaves in the same manner, men
standing on the ladders and scaffolding to catch
the tiles ; and, although the operation is done
with the rapidity of machinery, I have never seen
a drum or a tile drop from the hands of the catcher.

For the most part, the Christian quarter of
Smyrna, the largest portion of the city, is now
laid out with some regularity. The streets are
wider and better paved than formerly and lighted
with gas, and the houses are solidly constructed

of stone, somewhat after the Italian style, usually comprising two lofty stories. The large central hall of the ground-floor is checkered with blue-and-white marble, which is both cool and elegant in its effect. A pleasant Smyrniote custom is at evening for the family to sit at the open door and chat with their neighbors. On holidays, which are both numerous and carefully observed by the cessation of business, the doors and windows are "clustered with women," "all abroad to gaze," eating confectionery, and attired in stuffs of scarlet massively embroidered with silk and gold thread. In the jewelry they wear on such occasions the future husbands may see their dowries. On such a day many expressive and beautiful faces appear at the windows, particularly among the Greek women.

The society of Smyrna has the reputation of inclining to luxury and license. But the rose-conserves they offer the stranger are a very bewitching means of stopping the mouth of the critic, and turn the words of censure that fall from the lips of the moralist into laudatory phrases. In the month of roses, which of course is June, there as elsewhere, baskets heaped to the brim with rose-leaves are ranged in the fruit-bazaars, lading the air with perfume.

The rose-preserves are the result of a very simple process. To a pound of rose-petals add a pound of sugar; keep them over a slow fire until cooked ; then deposit them in a glass jar, and, under lock and key, guard them from prowling urchins seeking what they may devour. As occasion requires, have the sweetmeat served on a silver salver by a piquant Teniote maid.

The *baclavà* of Smyrna is another delicacy for which that city is famous ; it would soften the asperity of Timon of Athens. It is a flaky, diamond-shaped pastry, flavored with honey, almonds, and spices ; it melts on the tongue. During the Mohammedan holidays of Bairâm, or at Easter and the New Year, or a christening or a wedding, a large *tapsee* or circular pan of baclavâ is one of the indispensable delicacies of the occasion.

The *katymerry* is still another pastry prepared in Smyrna with peculiar excellence. Early in the morning men go about the streets crying, "Katymerria." It is eaten with coffee, in bed or immediately after rising.

The bakeries of Smyrna, as throughout the East, afford the observer much entertainment. The whole front of the shop is open summer and winter ; the broad counter, on which bread and pastry are kneaded and rolled, encroaches on the street and actually overhangs the pavement. Behind it the baker is busy, and before it, in the street, stands the customer purchasing loaves or eating katymerria. All the baking of the city, including meats, is done at the public bakery. The oven is behind the baker ; he lays the bread or meat on the red-hot floor with a long-handled shovel, which often projects far across the street, and sometimes hits a passer-by in the ribs, as the jolly, saucy, steaming baker flourishes it to and fro without regarding friend or foe. The loaves are carried on the shoulder through the streets in long, canoe-shaped troughs.

It is evident that the real fascinations of Smyrna are to be found not so much in what she possesses to remind us of the past as in the softness of her climate, and the peculiarly luxurious life of the inhabitants, who abandon themselves to the seduction of the air and scenery, and indulge in semi-Sybaritic habits adapted to what might be called their environment. Look, for example, at the plan of their country-houses. Adaptation, the first principle in architecture, we here find not only demonstrated, but contributing to the ease of the occupants. Most of these charming villas are built on one floor; a central or reception hall is surrounded by the apartments of the family. The house generally faces east and west; and this central room opens on two spacious porticoes profusely shaded by clambering vines laden with blossoms, and facing the grounds laid out with shade-trees and flowers. During the first half of the day the family occupy one portico; in the afternoon they move to the other side of the mansion. Thus they contrive to have shade and coolness during the whole day, and at evening they stroll forth under the stars.

At Smyrna we find ourselves fairly on the shores of the basin of the Mediterranean, which offers some of the most noted of the world's sanitariums. Were northerly winds prevalent, Smyrna could hardly be recommended as such. But, fortunately, during the warm months the prevailing winds are westerly and off the sea, and blow almost with the regularity of a trade-wind. The dampness of winter and the excessive heat of summer are objections to those who are not healthy; but from February until July the climate is very fine, and suited to many who suffer from chronic complaints.

In the outskirts of the city we find one of the choicest and most characteristic spots in the East —the celebrated Caravan Bridge.

In order to enjoy the attractions of this resort to the full one should repair to it early in the morning, while the figs are yet fresh and cold with dew, and breakfast there; or, better still, he should visit it when the sun approaches the west. Taking low stools by the water-side, and provided with the inevitable coffee and pipes, we are in a mood to yield ourselves to the seductive influences of this remarkable scene. An open space immediately around the river is devoted partly to the comfort of loungers, and partly to the encampment of groups of camels, which kneel in circles and receive their evening meal from their uncouth but picturesque drivers.

On one side of this space arise gardens of orange, mulberry, and pomegranate trees, echoing with the droning tune of the water-wheel by which they are irrigated. In another direction in solemn, stately majesty tower the marshaled host of cypresses which guard the Moslems' graves ; robed in muffling shadows of evening, their tapering crests, like points of spears, yet receive the parting glow of the sun. Beyond looms the Acropolis of the city, wearing on its brow the circle of crumbling battlements reared by the legions of Rome. The note of the turtle-dove falls plaintively but soothingly on the quietude of a scene which would give pleasure even to the soul of a pessimist. Around us, calmly smoking, Greeks, Armenians, Jews, and Franks are seated, chatting in groups ; and, nobler than them all, the much-maligned Turk, who in manners is still the finest gentleman of the age. The easy courtesy and stateliness of his mien have not been and never will be surpassed.

Across the Caravan Bridge, which spans the Meles at this place, we proceed to rural scenes so lovely that they have justly given to Smyrna the praise it bears.

This celebrated old city is girt by a circlet of hamlets of such simple pastoral beauty that he who has once tasted their attractions is never

satisfied until he can return and once more listen
to the slumberous monotone of the cicala in their
mulberry and linden groves, and hear the beat of
the tambourine under the vast umbrage of the
chenars of Bournâbashi, and there learn the quality
of the fruits of Smyrna, the finest in the world.
The grapes and figs of Smyrna, the melons of
Cassaba—match them who can! A stream me-
anders across the green of Bournâbashi, and loses
itself in the vineyard. Where the brook falls into
a basin under the sycamores, the peasant-girls,
white-armed and white-ankled, wash their clothes
singing, while the poppies are yet glistening with
the dew of the morning. The patriarchs of the
village smoke the narghilé hard by, in the shade
of the trellised vines ; and the wandering min-
strel earns a frugal meal with a rustic ditty.
There let me once more eat the figs and the
grapes of Smyrna and repeat the songs Anacreon
sung !

These villages are surrounded by barley-fields
and olive-groves, whose silver-gray leaves, turning a dark side upward when fluttering in the
wind, assume an indescribably soft, tender, poetic hue in the haze of the distant landscape.
There is no tree whose form seems so invested
with sentiment, whose gnarled, twisted, picturesque trunk, girt with gray-ribbed bark, like
a coat of mail, battered in many battles, so resembles a veteran who has seen life, and has a

career of struggling, suffering, and endurance to tell. Is it any wonder, then, that the ancients, when they discerned the humanity of the olive-tree, should have invented their fables of dryads or of nymphs turned into trees ?

The roads which lead to these villages around Smyrna, and the streams which course by them, as through the lovely valley of St. Ann's and the valley of Paradise, are bordered by oleander, laurel, and sweet-smelling myrtle, growing in the utmost profusion, and overarching the road, interwoven with the tamarisk and the round scarlet balls of the arbutus. Here and there, on knolls above the sea of verdure, or on the overhanging brow of a hill, a cluster of stone-pines seems to waft the music of the sea up to the mountains beyond, and gives a singular stateliness to the landscape as they wave away the years.

The romance of brigandage has given to these seemingly quiet and dreamful haunts a piquancy which really adds to the sentiment they inspire, such is the latent perversity that lurks in the human breast. I suppose a realist can analyze the poetry out of the most romantic bandit that ever lived. Granted ; and yet, after you have picked Milton's Satan to pieces, there is somehow an idea remaining that you have been juggled by the very clever casuist who has done it. We still have a lurking consciousness of the poetic aspects and uses of that magnificent creation. All the poetry

of the North American Indian has been analyzed
and sneered away by some. What then? The
fact remains nevertheless as true that there is
about the wild, stolid denizen of the Western
Plains a certain raciness and suggestiveness to
the fancy that still invests him with the garb of
romance.

I have seen some of those brigands of Smyrna.
They looked neither more nor less desperate than
many every-day people one meets constantly in
the streets, and their lives had doubtless often
been sufficiently prosy. But the daring, the defiance of law, the hair-breadth escapes, the mys-
teriousness of the life they led, were all so many
qualities that seemed to elevate them out of the
rank of your mere burglar or assassin. At present these rogues are not heard of so often as
formerly; but there was a time, not so long ago,
when even the villagers, I grieve to say, were in
league with them—let us hope out of fear rather
than villainy. Riches were then indeed a snare,
as the theologians tell us; for on their account
Smyrniotes of substance were entrapped and
kidnapped, and forced to purchase liberty with
heavy ransoms, or forfeit their lives. Yet those
were merry brigands withal, and many a good
story is told of the zest they showed in the country dances, selecting the prettiest maidens, and
occasionally alluring one of them to fly to the
mountains and become a robber's bride.

Brigandage, *par excellence*, although existing in remote districts of Asia Minor, had not yet become especially troublesome in the neighborhood of Smyrna, and gentlemen rode out daily to their country seats in the villages without fear of molestation. They hunted in the mountains at will, kept their gamekeepers, and looked for nothing more than a leopard, a wild boar, or a wolf, such as abound in Asia Minor in sufficient numbers to afford excellent sport. But, almost before they were aware, the Smyrniotes were aroused from their fancied security. Brigandage appeared in the vicinity so suddenly, and in so many quarters, that it almost seemed as if the brigands sprang armed out of the ground. Their organization was complete, as though it had proceeded from a preconcerted plan, devised by a number of associates. It is not likely, however, that it was more than a fortuitous aggregation of elements which naturally fell together, and only gradually gave expression to their communistic views regarding the nature of society. Robbers are only communists called by their right name : one is not more dangerous to society than the other, and both aim at that division of property which comes without labor or inheritance, or the application of the normal laws of supply and demand.

Now, these communists of Smyrna were not satisfied only with the vulgar mode of highway robbery known as the " stand-and-deliver " system.

Brigandage was raised by them to an intellectual rank—to a fine art. They studied the intricate problems of human nature, and, after discovering the points where it is most vulnerable, adroitly directed their attacks on the weak spot. A wealthy merchant of Smyrna would attract their analytical keenness of vision ; they discovered, by aid of their communistic principles, that he had no right to so large a share of money, even if won by brains and hard labor ; they decided that, although they had not the brains nor the love for work which could win wealth for them by ordinary methods, yet as men and brothers alone they had a right to share his wealth with him. After reaching this conclusion, the next thing was to put their views into execution. To kill this rich man would be very foolish ; that would be only slaughtering the goose that laid the golden eggs ; and, besides, his property would then be divided between the lawyers. It was to the advantage of the bandits that he should live as long as possible, but that meantime he should be tapped occasionally like a dropsical patient ; that is, that he should be relieved at intervals of some of his wealth. To play upon his fears would seem to be in his case the most feasible way to reach the desired result.

The art of writing letters was cultivated by them—letters couched in elegant style, offending none of the rules of syntax, and rich in figurative language, but at the same time direct, terse, and unmistakable in their meaning. Such letters the aforesaid merchant would receive sometimes, suggesting that a more equitable division of his property would be satisfactory to certain of his fellow citizens, who desired nothing more than a continued life of prosperity for him, but further observing that epidemics of a fatal character sometimes visited Smyrna, especially destructive in the upper crust of society, and that if he did not deposit the trifling sum of five thousand dollars in a certain place at a certain time, a mysterious Providence might visit him or his household with the epidemic.

With the beads of perspiration starting out on his brow, and a cold chill shivering down his spine, as if he already felt the poniard-like sharpness of the epidemic striking to his marrow, the merchant could devise no other remedy than to yield to these communistic sentiments; and at the appointed time a bag of five thousand dollars in gold would be found at the indicated rendezvous.

As a further means of gaining their public-spirited ends, these intelligent communists indoctrinated a large number of other citizens with their views, both in the city and in the neighboring villages. These citizens did not become actual brigands; that title and position were reserved for the leaders, the legislators, as it were, who expounded the principles of political economy for Asia Minor. But they assumed the honorary title of confederates or lobbymen, and wire-pullers, who aided the leaders by gaining information, concealing them in time of danger, entertaining them on festal nights, pointing out the geese that would bear plucking, conveying blackmailing correspondence, and making themselves generally useful in undermining the foundations of society for the purpose of furthering the success of communism, and at the same time wearing the mask of respectable citizenship until they could throw it off without risking their heads.

These confederates existed in all grades of society, and were especially numerous in the rural districts, so that it was sometimes exceedingly difficult to tell whom to trust ; often one would be surprised to learn that a neighbor or an acquaintance was a probable confederate. Suspicion increased, and the uneasiness of the community was well founded. It was more than a matter of report that the brigands came to the city on fête-days, and, dressed in Parisian styles, jauntily smoking cigarettes, and flourishing slender walking-sticks, actually visited the churches at the hour of mass. It was but too grave a certainty that they came down into the villages and actually danced with the servant-girls in the villas of the wealthiest citizens, who were consequently forced to remain in town during the summers. The caffegees or innkeepers were notoriously in league with the brigands.

Emboldened by the success of their communistic plans, the robbers finally seized the persons of influential Smyrniotes, without regard to their nationality, in order to bring about more speedily that equitable division of property so ardently desired by every public-minded communist. Turks when captured had their hearts torn out ; but the shedding of blood is not contrary to the communist code the world over. Other victims of the brigands were permitted, however, to have a certain time in which to redeem their lives by subscribing to the most advanced code of the nineteenth century so ably taught and practiced by the bandits of Smyrna. For example, the victim would be allowed twenty-four or forty-eight hours in which to raise a given sum of money for ransom. If the money came within the specified time, the brigands invariably released him ; for they were men of honor, and no bad faith was permitted to sully the lives of these apostles of the doctrine of the equitable division of property. But if the money did not arrive by the hour named, the prisoner lost an ear. Another day's delay deprived him of his other ear ; a third day showed him minus a hand, and the fourth day beheld him perhaps without a head. These diversions, doubtless devised to entertain the prisoner during his stay in the mountains, were varied to suit different cases, and in the mean time he was hurried from one den to another, in order that he

4

might not be rescued by the mistaken kindness of
the soldiers sent out by the Government.

A system of signals existed among this band
of jolly freebooters, which enabled them by day
or night to detect the approach of friend or foe.
A lookout would cry "Bah!" from a thicket like
a sheep. That meant friends. The crow of a
raven called for circumspection, the yelp of a fox
meant danger; and so on through a long list of
preconcerted signals.

Ears, hands, feet, piastres, and lives had now
been lost by a considerable number of unfortunates
who did not subscribe to the proletarian principles
of the brigands, and the Smyrniotes were beginning to think they had had about enough of this
doctrine, notwithstanding that there is nothing in
sociology so extraordinary as the long suffering
often shown by a people in enduring the preach-
ing and practice of the most destructive and pes-
tilent doctrines. But matters were brought to a
climax, and the city thrown into an uproar, when
news came that the Vice-Consul of Holland had
been seized by the brigands and carried off to the
mountains, and that a man was actually in the city
trying to raise a ransom of sixty thousand piastres, the sum which the brigands considered an
equitable share of the consular property. The
Vice-Consul had been captured at the very gate
of his garden, while accompanied by his children
and game-keepers. The ransom was finally raised

and taken to the mountains, and he was promptly released.

The brigands were, as before observed, men of their word, and, hard as it might be for them, they kept it even if it involved the violent death of their captive ; if a man's life was forfeited, they never flinched from performing their part of the contract, and sheared off his head without hesitation, although remorse might follow because they had not a little longer extended the time for his ransom. As good Christians also—good Oriental Christians—they were scrupulous in attending to the demands of religion. Greek priests they never harmed ; partly, perhaps, because monks have been occasionally known to be confederates and converts to the social principles of the brigands. But Roman Catholic priests, whom they considered as schismatics, have had their ribs tickled by the stilettos of the robbers. Their veneration for religion is also shown by the fact that when one of them was taken by the soldiers and confessed to his priest for absolution before his execution, his remorse was almost beyond pacifying because, once, when murdering a man on a Friday, some of the victim's blood had spurted into his mouth and he had swallowed it—a deadly sin because it was on a fast-day. No, even the devil must have his due, and to say that these brigands were not Christians would be—well, why should we be dragged into a theological snarl because we are talking about banditti? Farther in the interior, in Karamania or Kurdistan, the robbers are generally Mohammedans, and these remarks would not apply to them.

That nerve and unswerving rectitude in the pursuit of their plans were characteristic of these brigands, is illustrated by the fearful initiation of one of their number into this society of select and kindred spirits. His name was Yanni or John, and he was gamekeeper to a Turkish gentleman, who was the unfortunate possessor of an ambitious wife and a very beautiful daughter, who fell desperately in love with the handsome gamekeeper; he returned her passion, and several clandestine meetings resulted in leaving her in an interesting condition. About this time the lovers discovered that her mother was weary of her lord, and regarded their amour with favor. In the mean time Yanni had formed a pleasant and instructive acquaintance with some of the brigands, who had made him a convert to their socialistic principles. "There seemed to be a providence in it," as some would say. When a woman loves passionately and desperately, she can be converted to almost any belief by the man she loves; and so Yanni found when he discussed the matter with Zeineb. She entered readily into his plans, and her mother easily became an accomplice. A quieting dose was administered to the poor, credulous, unsuspecting, uxorious Turk, given to him in his coffee

by his tender and affectionate wife. He passed
away to the paradise of the houris, and the two
women and Yanni now robbed his coffers at leisure, and started off to the mountain den where he
had agreed to meet the brigands. It was among
the wild ranges of Tachtalee. About midnight
the party arrived there, and found the banditti
around a fire in a cave, wrapped in their capotes,
but on the alert because the lookout had announced
approaching footsteps. Having returned the preconcerted signal, Yanni and the women were ad-
mitted to the presence of the chief, who extended
a gruff welcome to Yanni, but fiercely demanded
who the women were. On being informed, the
chief swore with fearful imprecations that no Moslem dogs should pollute the camp with their presence, so long as there were so many fair Christian
women from whom the brigands could select their
paramours. In terms which could not be mistaken, he informed Yanni that his admission as
a member of the band depended on his killing
Zeineb without a moment's delay ; any hesitation
could only result in the forfeiture of his own
as well as of her life ; and, suiting the action to
the word, the chief placed a pistol in his hand.
Yanni's principles were equal to the occasion.
Heeding not the frantic screams of the girl, who
clasped his knees in desperate appeal, he leveled
the muzzle of the pistol at her head and fired ;
at the same instant the dagger of the chief pierced

her mother to the heart, and the two corpses were thrown over the cliff. Having thus proved himself to be made of the right metal, Yanni was now heartily welcomed by the band, and, after a long course of adventure, became their leader. Captured at last by the soldiery, he bribed his keeper to let him escape from prison on the eve of execution ; but he was finally killed in a skirmish with the troops.

One of the most interesting occasions in the career of these brigands was the waylaying and murder of *the Tartar* and the capture of the treasure in his charge. Except on the two or three short railways, the mail is carried in Turkey by men called Tartars, probably because they were originally Turks of unmixed Tartar extraction, who could be depended on for their fidelity, courage, and endurance. They ride on fleet horses at a gallop day and night, accompanied by one or two men, and armed to the teeth. When they arrive at an inn, whatever be the hour, everything has to give way to them. A hasty meal and pipes are at once prepared, and then, rolling themselves in their capotes, the Tartar and his attendants snatch a few rapid winks on the divan, and are off again on a fresh relay of horses.

A ride of this sort from Bagdad to Constantinople is attended with great exhaustion, and could be endured as a business only by men specially trained to it. When traveling in Asia Minor, I have repeatedly been aroused at midnight by the bustle and noise attending the arrival of the Tartar. But the inns where he stops are often kept by men who are in league with the brigands, who are thus thoroughly informed of the probable amount of treasure he carries in his saddle-bags, or of any other travelers who may repay the risk of capture.

The brigands of Smyrna made the lives of these Tartars exceedingly uncertain. There are many narrow defiles which have, in the course of years, become known as haunts frequented by the robbers ; and there, behind the rocks, they would lie in ambush. As the Tartar rushed by on a dark, stormy night, the flash of muskets would suddenly illumine the gloom. Sometimes a fatal shot would fell him and his horse to the ground ; sometimes he would escape, to lose his life perhaps on another occasion from the same peril.

But long success at length gave a rash audacity to the attempts of the robbers, which, for the time, brought matters to a crisis. The capture of the Dutch Vice-Consul led the Turkish Government to see that, in order to avoid foreign complications, it must bestir itself ; and a new governor was sent to Smyrna, with a force sufficient to exterminate the brigands, and stamp out the flames of communism. The robbers were forced to disband before an energy which, if spasmodic, was at least effectual for the time. Some

of them even suffered martyrdom for their principles, and died as the dog dieth.   Caught in
some cases through the guidance of the confederates who turned against them in the hour of
adversity, they were cuffed, beaten, kicked, and
called by every obscene epithet with which the
Oriental languages abound, and, with their arms
tightly pinioned, were driven through the streets
of Smyrna, followed by jeering multitudes.   In a
square, or where four streets met, a noose was
placed around their necks, and they were hoisted
to the eaves of a shop, and left there for the city
to gaze at them, and the birds of the air to pick
out their eyes.

For several years after this a certain quiet
reigned in Smyrna.   But whenever the Government relaxes its vigilance the brigands are liable
to make their appearance in the neighborhood.

SCIO.

If you climb the mountains behind Bournâbashi, you will see an isle, beyond the Bay of
Smyrna, that beckons us to its shores with perpetual charms.   The Genoese called it Fior di
Levante, and we to-day know it as Scio's rocky
isle.

From Smyrna one may reach Scio by steamer,
or, if he prefers, by one of the curious coasting

craft, which seem to reproduce some of the peculiarities of ancient galleys in their quaint construction.

There is a strait nine miles wide on the coast of Ionia. On one side is Teos, where Anacreon sung of love and wine long ago. Opposite Teos stretches the spiny ridge of Scio's isle, reposing on the perfect waters of the Ægean. Its crags and vine-clad slopes are suffused with that indescribable roseate hue that invests the landscapes of the East, and dreamily suggests strange attractions, of which the traveler has but a faint conception until he has landed and dwelt there a space, and become familiar with the inexhaustible variety of her beauty.

The plan of this islet is simple enough. A central ridge intersects it north and south, and gives emphasis to the softness of the scenery. The lower slopes and plains along the seaside are enriched with luxuriant vegetation, which is rendered picturesque by the Italian architecture of the villas scattered over the island, and the peaked roofs of the huts of the peasantry. A landing is effected at Port Kastro, on the eastern side. This is the only town of consequence on the island.

It is a matter of more importance than many are aware of that the approach to a place we see for the first time should be agreeable, in order that the welcome our spirits and fancy receive should seize us by the heart, and make us feel

already at home ere we are fairly arrived. Those
who are unaccustomed to analyze their mental
operations find it difficult to understand how
much this first impression has to do with our
final estimate of a place, although it is true we
may thus not unfrequently misjudge a locality
which shows great attractions on further acquaintance. Scio has fortunately all the qualifications
essential to steal and to hold the heart of the
stranger on his first arrival, if repose and amenity of scenery are what he seeks.

The ship, slipping idly down the coast, past
the group of islands called the Spalmadores, suddenly opens the entrance to a small landlocked
basin of a port. On the right frowns a Genoese
fortress with gray pepper-box turrets, on which
flutters the crimson banner of the Crescent. On
the left is a low range of hills crested by a row
of somnolent windmills perpetually turning their
whirring white arms against the sky. Before us
lies the town, whose wharves are picturesque with
the shipping loading gayly-colored fruits that are
piled in glowing masses. The houses are partially concealed by a skirmish-line of coffee-shops
and market-booths, where the idlers of an idle
day while away the idle hours with the seductive
chibouque. What little activity is evident about
the port is of exactly a sort to intensify the narcotic effect of a scene that is bathed in the vapory
haze of a dreamful summer's day.

We go on shore, and pass beyond the sight of the port into dark cool lanes lined with massive mansions of stone. Our first call is the signal of a welcome, attended by the unfailing refreshments of rose or mastic conserves served by a charming Sciote damsel, and followed by the inevitable chibouque.

In the absence of hotels, the stranger has taken in advance a villa in the Campo, and now proceeds to inspect and occupy it. "John, fetch the mules!" The mules are led up; they are fine animals, sleek, well saddled, and docile for mules. A ride of four or five miles into the country results in leaving the newly arrived traveler in a state of rapture bordering on imbecility.

On leaving Port Kastro one enters the Campo, an irregular plain on the eastern side of Scio, stretching to the mountains, and fringed by the yellow sands of a beach kissed by the silver foam of the Ægean, beyond whose waves loom the faint roseate ranges of Anatolia. The Campo is covered with the most luxuriant gardens, orange plantations, and trellised graperies, each of which is entered through a stately gateway, surmounted by a summer-house and a porter's lodge. Over the gate are sculptured the armorial bearings of a family perhaps long since passed away, and on entering the grounds the visitor sees before him an elegant dwelling of cut stone, whose second story, where the owner resides, is approached by a noble stairway, protected by a massively elegant balustrade. The windows and doors are all surmounted by archivolts of different-colored stones. The spacious, marble-floored apartment gives a deliciously cool and hospitable aspect to the mansion ; a divan is spread between the windows, and the breeze, which bears to us the moan of the sea, also wafts into the halls the subtile fragrance of jasmines, syringas, and roses, and the honeyed scent of the linden's pendulous, plume-like blooms.

From the flat, parapeted roof one gazes at evening over a landscape touched with the tenderest of hues, and inclosed by the amethyst of the sea. As the twilight comes on, and the argent disk of the full moon looms, a white fire, above the slumbering groves, diffusing a pale golden haze over the enchanted isle, the hoot of the owl adds to the sentiment of the hour, and the nightingale's improvisations increase the fervor of our enthusiasm, and lend rapture to the splendor of a night in paradise.

Oh the beauty and the glory of those landscapes of Scio! Oh the softness of the clime, never too warm or too cool! When did we tire of the loveliness that surrounded us? When did the time pass wearily? Never! Our stay there was like a long dream of delight, an unbroken reverie, in a land where we fed on the lotus and drank the waters of Lethe ; never before, never since, have I passed two months of

such unalloyed happiness as the days that glided
so quietly away on Scio's isle. In the morning
we roved among orange-groves or galloped by the
seaside ; we had our siesta at noonday, bathed in
the sea at sunset, then watched the moon looming
above the Scian shore, and then lay down to pleasant dreams.

Often in our morning rides we met the peasant
maids in picturesque costume, spinning as they
rode or walked, with the shuttle under the left
arm, and holding the thread and spindle in the
right hand, as described by Homer in the Iliad.
Not unfrequently we saw a woman mounted on a
mule, singing lullaby to an infant at the breast,
while another child sat behind her on the long
saddle, and still another curly-headed urchin clung
to the crupper, while the rude tinkle of the mule-
bell chimed with the sportive voices of the children and the crooning song of the mother.

Mules are chiefly used as beasts of burden in
Scio, and riding is the habit of all. "If wishes
were horses, then beggars might ride," is an old
proverb which is literally interpreted in this curious island ; for even the beggars came to our
gate on borrowed mules.

There is an element which adds a singular interest, a quiet pathos, to all one sees in Scio. Not
all of the giddy multitudes who hurry by the
Place de la Concorde at Paris forget what scenes
that center of gay festivities beheld when it was

the site of the guillotine during the Reign of Terror. Through all the pomp and revelry of to-day
the pensive mind yet hears the wail of that epoch
of blood, that shall echo down the ages while time
endures, as silent but as loud and persistent as the
voice of conscience. And thus it is at Scio. Go
where you will, eat, drink, and be merry, drain
the goblet to the lees, until the fancy is intoxi-
cated with the mild beneficence of the elixir of its
clime, with the splendor of its scenery and the
eyes of its maidens, black as night and perilous as
fire, that shake the soul with longing and despair ;
yet evermore, like the slave at the elbow of the
triumphing Cæsar, stands the genius of the isle,
where she can whisper : "What recks it all? Give
me back my lost wealth, my sons and daughters
swept away by the torch and the sword ! "

Ah ! that is the mystery that broods over it
all, the memory of that terrible desolation and
doom that befell Scio in the Greek Revolution—
a horror which there are yet some who have sur-
vived to repeat the story of the wildest tragedy
of the nineteenth century.

Before ever the Turks came, ages ago, the
Genoese had captured and beautified the isle.
They introduced their customs and their architecture, and noble blood ran in the veins of many
of the proud Italians. There are still Justiniani
in Scio who remind us of what was once one of
the most noted names of the Mediterranean.

But, after the splendor of their dominion had
endured for centuries, a fleet of the Ottomans,
under the great Pialee, anchored in the roads,
the banner of the Genoese was lowered, and the
Turk took possession of the Fior di Levante,
and made it an appanage of the Sultana Validé
or Queen Mother of the Empire. It is to the
latter cause that the island owes the fact that,
with one exception, it has been treated with a
leniency that enabled Scio, before the revolution,
to reach a position of wealth and intelligence un-
equaled by any other subject provinces of the
Turks.

When the revolution broke out the Sciotes
refrained from hostilities, and were unmolested,
until some turbulent Samians came over and laid
siege to the Turkish garrison at Port Kastro.
This naturally infuriated the Moslems, and, be-
lieving or assuming that the inoffensive Sciotes
had invited the Samians over, a fleet and an
army were sent against the doomed island. At
that time there was a flourishing university at
Port Kastro, and the population of Scio numbered over one hundred thousand. But, after
the Turkish hordes had ravaged the island and
massacred the people, not above twenty - five
thousand remained, the rest had been murdered
or carried into slavery, and there was scarcely a
villa that had not been more or less injured by
the fury of the assailants. Three thousand were

burned or suffocated in the Convent of St. Minas alone, and almost every house is haunted by a tragedy of its own that is full of pathos and horror.

When the Greeks had recovered from their first grief at the narrative of the sufferings of Scio, a cry of vengeance arose from the nation. Large sums were contributed for the fitting out of a naval armament, and the ports of Spezzia, Hydra, and Psarra, resounded with the din of preparation. Soon a confederate fleet, command- ed by Miaulis, whose strength lay rather in the valor and skill of its seamen than the number or size of its vessels, was seen cruising around the island, reconnoitering the enemy's station. On the night of the 18th Kara Ali proclaimed an im- posing festival throughout his fleet in view of the expected appearance of the new moon, which he was destined never again to behold. But while the Turks were wasting their time in rioting, the Greeks had matured, and were now preparing to execute, a terrible plan of retribution. Constan- tine Kanaris, a youth of Psarra, boldly volunteered with George Pepinis, of Hydra, to conduct two fire-ships into the very midst of the enemy's lines, which now included thirty-eight sail. A band of chosen seamen manned the brigs, with which on the 18th they started on their perilous undertaking, escorted by four other vessels that were to keep in the vicinity, and pick up the *brulôtiers* when they betook themselves to their launches.

The brigs beat across the southern mouth of the strait, under false colors. As evening set in, a portentous gloom overhung the deep, but the night was tranquil, only a fresh land breeze shaking the shrouds of the Turkish armada which lay a league from the shore. At midnight the brigs wore ship, and stood up the channel, until they found themselves in the midst of the enemy. Kanaris's *brulôt* grappled the huge bulk of the flag-ship. He touched the train, and as he pushed off in his open barge, gave the battle-cry of the ancient hosts of imperial Byzantium, " Victory to the Cross ! " which at that solemn hour rang on the ear of the startled foe like his death-knell. Pepinis sought to fire the rear-admiral's two-decker, but, before the flames had been effectually communicated, the *brulôt* swung off, and, driving through the fleet, an object of terror, set fire to a third line-of-battle ship. Both of the latter vessels, though saved for the present, were rendered unfit for future service.

While these scenes were enacting, in other quarters of the roadstead, Kara Ali's magnificent three-decker presented a sublime and appalling spectacle. The roaring flames, leaping from spar to spar, enveloped the noble vessel from truck to the water's edge in one vast sheet of fire ; the ruddy glow tinged the lurid heavens

5

to such an extent that the horror-smitten inhabitants of Smyrna many miles distant, waking up at midnight, saw above the mountains which overhung their port a crimson light in the southwestern sky like the radiance which in the east betokens the approach of day. To add to the solemnity of the scene above the thunder of the rushing flames and the screams of the dying, arose the deep boom of the doomed vessel's carronades which went off one by one, as they were successively reached by the conflagration, like minute guns, fired to celebrate the obsequies of those who perished on that memorable night.

At two o'clock in the morning the flag-ship blew up. The vessel contained twenty-two hundred and eighty-six souls, of whom only one hundred and eighty reached the shore alive. The commanders of the various ships of the fleet were lost ; and Kara Ali himself, as he was escaping from the burning hulk, was mortally wounded by a falling timber, and expired at daybreak.

Little by little Scio has recovered from the hurricane of war, but has not yet reached its former population or wealth. And one can easily perceive what a melancholy interest is added to the beauty of the villas and the scenery, when he meets survivors of that appalling catastrophe, and hears them relate in moving accents the story of the scenes they saw with their own eyes.

Still, like others, the people can not always sup on horrors, and something of their old-time gayety survives, and gives life to the merriment of their gala-days, which are many. Each village has its special festival, each saint his holiday. The vintage and the harvest also have their wassail and dances, where one can imagine that the spirit of Anacreon or of grand old Homer still presides. Is not this the isle of Homer? and lo, there on its western shore still cluster the peasant-huts of Volisso, reputed for over three thousand years to be the residence of the blind bard. Is not that enough? Has any one the daring to fly in the face of such a hoary tradition?

The most picturesque festival of Scio is the Eve of St. John. It is celebrated with fireworks, bonfires, and the crack of old muskets, which give a singular animation to the scenery. Before every house ring the strains of timbrel and guitar, and the blithe songs of the dancers, until a late hour.

The quaintest and most picturesque portion of Scio is the mastic district called Sclavia, which extends from St. Minas to the southern extremity of the isle. The surface is more broken than the Campo, and the hamlets of the peasantry are curiously grouped in the hollows or on the hillsides. The old moss-covered stone-huts are sometimes joined together by roofs solidly constructed over

dark lanes, while here and there an old-time tower
or villa rises grandly above the landscape ; sometimes a stately avenue of cypresses leads up to a
venerable mansion, where an equally venerable
steward will repeat the tragedy of the place with
a dramatic pathos that lives in the memory long
after one has left the isle.

From the heights of Sclavia are seen the outlines of Samos and Icaria, melting into the vapory
offing of the Ægean, and recalling many a fair legend that causes the fancy to kindle and the heart
to beat with enthusiasm.

It is in the mastic cantons that the lentisk
grows so abundantly as to supply the island with
a large share of its revenue. Most of the gum-
mastic which appears in the boudoir of the Oriental lady, or is employed to flavor cordials, is
gathered from the trees of Sclavia. The pistachio
also grows abundantly in Scio, and the almonds
of the island are exceptionally fine.

Do people ever die in Scio nowadays of aught
but old age ? Doubtless ; but they have an unusually good opportunity of living there longer
than in many other parts of the globe, for the
wind, from whichever quarter it blows, comes directly off the sea, and is laden with tonic qualities. It must be conceded that the position of the
mountains is such as to allow the raw northerly
winds full sweep during the winter season. In-
clement days are, therefore, not infrequent at

that time, while the construction of the houses is adapted rather for warm than cold weather. But I am convinced that from March until June, inclusive, and from September until November, the invalid can derive great benefit from the pure, temperate, and delicious air of Scio, and thus perhaps add materially to the length of his days.

NAPLES.

WHEN we sail westward from Scio, and, threading the Straits of Messina, arrive at Naples, and are told that it was founded by the nymph Parthenope, we are reduced to the dilemma either of accepting the actuality of at least one nymph, which would carry the whole question of mythology, or of denying that Naples was ever founded at all. However, leaving aside all such archæological questions, we find there not only the choicest spot in Hesperia, but also that, like most of the world's paradises, its amazing wealth of attractions receives a tone from the sea which caresses its shores, but eludes it when it seeks to inclose it in a lasting embrace. Amethyst and turquoise are the colors of the sea around the shores of Naples—amethyst verging to purple as its surface fades off to meet the sky, and turquoise when we look into its depths. The curving, sickle-like Bay of Naples resembles a circlet of emerald and gold inclosing lapis lazuli, and like an annular ring surmounted at the head by the cone of Vesuvius blazing at night like a magnificent ruby. When one gazes at the flames shooting skyward or rolling liquid fire to the sea, he finds it difficult to imagine that, when Spartacus led the gladiators to revolt against Rome, he made his headquarters in the crater of Vesuvius, which at that time had been dormant from immemorial ages, and was overgrown with forest and underwood.

Such is the expanse of the sail-flecked Bay of Naples, that the city, except when one is near to it, forms but an inconsiderable object in the landscape, which thus depends for its effect chiefly upon the superb coloring of natural objects and the symmetrical combination of lines toward one common center—the towering cone of Vesuvius, which rises first by a long, gentle slope, and terminates somewhat abruptly by a more rapid ascent near the summit.

The majestic stone-pines that cluster on the projecting crags or shade the grounds of many a romantic villa, and the vineyards thriving on the volcanic soil, add variety and beauty to a scene that has the inestimable quality of growing on one's esteem, like the gradually approaching parallels of a besieging army, until it carries our enthusiasm by storm. Like Cleopatra, "age can not wither, time can not stale its infinite variety."

The perpetually shifting scenes of life among the people, the picturesqueness of the native craft, gayly carved and painted, and the number of excursions that may be made to adjacent places of interest—Baiæ or Capri, Pompeii, Salerno, Posilippo, Sorrento—all aid to render Naples a charming resort, in winter and spring, especially from February until May. In those entrancing days one may well declare that false was he who first said, " See Naples and then die " ; for, once it is seen, one burns with the desire to live. Who talks of dying with such superb prospects in view, such a soft, delicious air fanning his temples and holding this wonderful lachrymæ christi at his lips ? What a clime is this, when even the volcano that destroys cities condescends to grow such a vintage on the sides of its precipices of lava !

When summer comes, however, we are reminded that the city of Naples can be in no sense a health resort during the hot season. In no city of Europe is population so densely packed together as in the capital of Campania. Its teeming multitudes swarm like bees in a hive. For the large majority poverty is the common lot, and many thousands live in the most abject squalor. The filth of some quarters of the city is beyond description, while the sewers emptying into the port directly in front of the Marino or seaside promenade, called the Villa Reale, pollute the

air and reek with pestilential stenches. The picturesqueness of the lower orders in Naples is emi-
nently and essentially the picturesqueness of dirt,
so eloquently apostrophized by Mr. Ruskin.

Your eater of macaroni, lying in the sun, the
incarnation of indolence, the lazzaroni who dive
in the harbor for pennies, or sleep in the streets
without a roof over them at night, and carry a
countless population on their backs, may be artis-
tically interesting in cool weather; but when the
broiling days of August arrive, and the rage of
the dog-star, then hail the trim felucca, spread
her white wings, and speed to Capri.

And this leads us to observe the real value of
the Bay of Naples as a residence: it is because
of the many charming spots within easy distance
from the city to which the tourist or the invalid
may resort—places not only of great historic interest, like Pompeii, but of extraordinary loveliness, like the orange-groves of Castellamare, or the
fairy isle of Capri, lying off the end of the southern horn of the Bay of Naples, and acting somewhat as a breakwater against southwesterly gales.
About nine miles in circumference, a mere limestone rock, it yet offers within its narrow limits
scenery of great beauty, variety, and grandeur,
and a climate that is beneficial to all except invalids so far affected by phthisis that they find
the northerly winds too vigorous even in that
balmy latitude; for, as the south side of Capri is

a tremendous perpendicular precipice, falling hundreds of feet to the blue sea far below, it is very difficult to find a site that is not exposed to those winds.

The ruins of the palace and baths of Tiberius still remain on Capri, where he passed the last years of his life in debaucheries that have become proverbial. Here, in this elysium, where one would think the serene purity of the surrounding sea would have an elevating influence, this tyrant lived in a manner that dwells to this day in the memory of the islanders like a dream of the Inferno. As one saunters over the lovely, sunlit, vine-clustered crags of Capri, or reposes under the greenery of the trellised terraces, gazes over the quivering azure of the mysterious sea, fading off to unknown lands under the heat of a southern sun, and listens to the tinkle of the goat-bells among the rocks in the calmness of the sunset hour, he wonders why the memory of foul deeds should so linger to pollute some of earth's fairest scenes.

The blue grotto of Capri is justly famous; the exquisite tint of the water under the rocks touches the emotions like a delicate strain of music. I remember a similar phenomenon, that is less known and visited, in a cave near Cabo Giram, on the southern coast of Madeira. The Devil's Hole, at Bermuda, is another instance. In each case the phenomenon is doubtless caused by the great

evaporation produced by steady heat, aided perhaps by the absence of high tides, thus resulting
in an increase of the saline density of the water.
Although the blue in the color of water may be,
and doubtless is, sometimes due to other causes,
it is now a well-known fact that the azure of sea-
water is generally in proportion to the quantity of
salt it holds in solution.

Those who are fond of quails, fresh, tender,
and savory, may find their appetite for this sort
of game gratified at Capri, whither those birds
are wafted by the southerly spring winds, and
wearily alight for rest. Too many of them find
it there in the net or the gun of the fowler, and
never get beyond Capri. With them it is literally, "See Naples and then die."

CORSICA.

CORSICA looms grandly above the sea, her
lofty mountains capped with eternal snows and
rosy-red at sunset, a truly magnificent spectacle.
The weather was fine the first time I approached
it, and the white lateen sails of the large fishing-
boats and the scarlet caps of the fishermen admirably harmonized with the deep blue of the
sea, and, as a foreground, greatly assisted the imagination in grasping an idea of the grandeur of

the ranges soaring in the interior of the island to a height of nearly ten thousand feet.

This was on approaching by the Straits of Maddalena, although Corsica, everywhere mountainous, looms up sternly from all sides, faced with vast granitic precipices, seamed by tartarean gorges, and clothed with dense forests of chestnut, and on the upper crags with larch and fir. It fitly seems the birthplace of him who shook the world with the stupendous power of his intellect, for there Napoleon Bonaparte was born. It is a curious circumstance, which nobody seems to have observed, that on the opposite side of the strait, on the northern end of Sardinia, and directly facing Corsica, is an enormous rock pedestaled on a cliff, and shaped like a striding bear. Was it not a bear, the bear of Russia, that overthrew the power of Napoleon?

This mighty soldier seems by the law of selection to have been *deduced from* the long, sturdy struggles of the Corsicans. After centuries of resistance to Genoese and Gaul, and internecine strife among their mountain fastnesses, the Corsicans at last produced Napoleon. Those who make a philosophical study of the development of man do not seem to have given the attention one might expect to an investigation of the ethnic laws that operated in the rise of the Napoleonic dynasty. Here, on a small island, concrete and distinct in its history, ample opportunity is offered for examining into the laws which develop great intellects.

The Corsicans themselves are well aware of the importance of the subject. They are all familiar with the events in the career of the great Corsican ; they all arrogate to themselves a share in his glory, and boldly assume that it was not France that conquered Corsica, but that they have taken France ; for it was the thoroughly Corsican son of a companion of Paoli who so long resisted the inroads of the French, that raised France out of the ruins of the Revolution to a new life, founded the empire, and at thirty-four mounted the throne which he had created for a nation that he found soaked in blood and smoking with the lurid embers of the Revolution.

Indeed, so earnestly do the spirited islanders identify themselves with the founder of the empire, that almost every shepherd tending his tawny flock on the mountains, almost every little shopkeeper of Ajaccio or Calvi, will assure you that he is connected with the family of the Emperor. This pride in Napoleon took a novel form early in the century. Aided by an English fleet and army, Paoli, after many years' exile, returned to his native isle in 1795, and so successfully attacked the French garrisons in several of the seaports, that the Corsicans rose *en masse* against the hated yoke of France, and their representatives assembled at Corte, then the capital of Corsica, unanimously voted to exchange the oppressive rule of the French for the protection of Great Britain, and accepted Lord Minto as viceroy. But, when the exploits of Bonaparte rang over Europe, the Corsicans hastened to renew their allegiance to France, and the British made the best of a bad job by evacuating the island. Since that time there has been no further question about the authority of France in Corsica.

There is no doubt that the foreign rule of so able and enterprising, and, on the whole, well-regulated a people as the French, has been of very great advantage to Corsica. Until they exchanged the Genoese for the French domination, the Corsicans were in some respects closely allied to barbarism. Little or no effort to improve their island was attempted. Few or no roads existed; the vast abundance of the annual harvest of chestnuts easily provided all with at least a subsistence; and commerce was confined almost entirely to the coral fisheries.

The French have opened roads that entirely surround the island, and are projecting a railway along the eastern coast from Bastia to Bonifacio. On that side of Corsica the mountains are low and calcareous, and in the course of ages the rains have washed down the soil to the sea and produced a low alluvial plain several miles wide, extending almost the whole length of the island.

This alluvial strip is crossed by streams and covered in places by marshes and feverish lakes, and reeks with miasma. But it is the only really unwholesome district in Corsica.

The western half of the island is of granitic formation, terminating at the coast in abrupt and frowning precipices grooved by tremendous gorges, and rising in the interior to such heights as Monte Rotondo and Monte d'Oro, respectively 9,246 and 8,720 feet above the level of the sea. On the summit of the former are two small lakes of great depth. Near the center of Corsica is an elevated table-land, where the capital was situated in former ages. The map of Corsica suggests the back of a tortoise. The configuration of the mountains resembles the laminations of the shell, and the long promontory of Cape Corso at the northern end is not unlike the head and neck of the reptile projecting beyond the shell, and taking a cautious survey of the environing seas.

But in nothing has the firm, orderly rule of the French in Corsica been more apparent and beneficial than in the suppression of the terrible code of the vendetta, and the brigandage which resulted from it, and prevented the improvement of the island. It pervaded all classes, and for ages had kept society in a state verging on extreme barbarism. The occasional deeds of heroism, the occasional picturesque and romantic incidents which attended this savage custom, were but a slight palliation for a system that brooded over the island like a fatal blight.

In many half-civilized communities, in which the regular practice of organized legal authority seemed insufficient for the protection of the individual from insult and injury, it has too often been more or less a half-permitted custom for individuals to take the law into their own hands, and assert by violence their right to immunity from attack. But this has naturally resulted in persistent attempts at revenge, as both parties in such cases consider themselves in the right. Hence results a feud between families or communities, lasting sometimes for generations. When once established and tacitly approved by society, there is no custom that is more difficult to eradicate; for the highest sentiment of a community, that of honor, is perverted in its favor; and what began originally as a crime, winked at by the people owing to palliating circumstances, becomes in the end almost a duty demanded of him who would preserve the respect of the circle in which he moves. This is well illustrated by the continuance of lynch law in some of our best-regulated States, the wicked immunity too often allowed to the murderer who avenges marital infidelity by the revolver rather than by resorting to courts of justice, and the long and bloody family feuds which are yet quite too frequent among some

of the best families of the Southern States of
America.

Among the Arabs the vendetta has been a
strong social characteristic. It existed until recently in the south of Greece, and I have known
of men remaining concealed there for ten years
in their own houses or towers, without even ven-
turing forth except on the back of a woman. Thus
alone could they hope to escape the musket of the
avenger, who, without any abatement of vigilance,
watched and thirsted for their blood. The vin-
dictiveness of the Albanians continues to this day
to be almost a byword in the Levant, and men of
that race who have an injury to avenge have been
thrown into prison sometimes on a trumped-up
charge by those who had given the cause of offense, and have been kept confined a lifetime by
bribing the jailer. I considered myself very fortunate, after a fight with one of these revengeful
ruffians, in being able to leave the place a few
weeks later, and thus keeping my heart safe inside of my ribs.

But nowhere has the institution of the vendetta
been more thoroughly organized and accepted as
a social custom, and nowhere has it been eradicated with more difficulty, than in Corsica. This
tacit code, accepted by the local traditions of centuries, was as bloody as the laws of Draco. All
offenses were liable to be washed out in blood,
according to the disposition of the one offended.

The women as well as the men took the law into their own hands. They not only incited their male relations to avenge any injuries done to them, but also too often murdered their enemies themselves. The seducer who failed to fulfill his promises of marriage knew too well what to expect ; and the woman who thus avenged herself was regarded as a heroine, and ballads were composed which recited the bravery she had displayed.

The time is coming when it will be understood the world over that murder is crime under all circumstances except self-defense ; and that in cases of seduction, whether the woman be married or single, the fault is no less hers than her partner's, and to deal out death to him alone is an unjust division of penalty. Women are free agents ; and if men are more aggressive, women, on the other hand, have in their power stronger motives for resistance to temptation.

At any rate, in Corsica, after a man had been assassinated, for whatever cause, his family assumed as a duty the avenging of his death ; and a vendetta or family feud began, which lasted so long as any male remained alive on either side. As every one went armed, reprisal was liable at any moment. Laborers sought their fields with dread, not knowing but that their enemy was lurking behind the next bush. Others concealed themselves in the upper story of their stone houses, protecting the staircase with an iron door perfo-

rated with loopholes, through which they could
shoot an approaching enemy. One unfortunate
victim proscribed by this terrible code remained
thus for fifteen years in his house. At last he
was told that his enemy had left the ambush for
a few hours and gone to the city. Taking a long
breath of relief, the forlorn prisoner once more
stepped forth outside of his door, and trod the
earth with the unutterable satisfaction of one who
unexpectedly gains his freedom after a period of
hopeless bondage. Again, at least for a while, he
was a free man. Nature looked joyous, and his
heart leaped once more with the exhilaration of his
younger days. But at that moment a ball pierced
his bosom. The avenger of fifteen years had not
relaxed his vigilance, and his long waiting was re-
paid at last.

What sort of society is this, in which such
things are not only permitted but approved?
And yet there are some in our country who by
their actions almost make one think they would
import to this happy land one of the most atro-
cious relics of a savage life that have come down
to our century to give us a glimpse of what those
good old times were of which some pessimists
have so much to say.

In this small island, with only the population
of a moderate-sized city, the assassinations in
thirty years alone reached the enormous figure of
4,300. A natural result of the vendetta was the

creation of one of the most remarkable systems of brigandage ever known. Many of those who avenged their honor by assassination, instead of betaking themselves for shelter to their houses, escaped to the mountains, where they lived on game or chestnuts of the forest, with occasional supplies covertly furnished them by their friends. They haunted the caves of the highest mountains in bands, and as a rule only attacked travelers for actual robbery when urged by pinching necessity. Thus a community averaging upward of a thousand men, every one of whom was a murderer, was permanently withdrawn from the able-bodied producers of Corsica, and acted as a terror to enterprise, and openly defied all attempt to reduce them to order. Public opinion, it must be owned, was entirely to blame for this wretched state of affairs ; for the brigands were considered respectable men, who had been brought to this condition through the misfortune, entirely beyond their control, as was assumed, of practicing the bloody code of the vendetta.

After many abortive attempts to crush both the vendetta and its corollary—brigandage—in Corsica, the French Government finally decided to stamp out this accursed system, by measures of the most uncompromising and decisive character. Not only was every assassin and brigand executed as soon as captured, as a common miscreant, but a law was passed and rigidly enforced

making it a penal offense for any one to carry
arms of any description, not excepting such as desired merely to follow the chase. This law was
only slightly relaxed after the outrages it was
intended to prevent had been rendered infamous
and nearly extinguished. Another law was also
most rigidly enforced, which came home to the
whole community; it was the law of conceal-
ment, which rendered every one liable to impris-
onment who was known to aid or harbor any
brigand or assassin. Whole families were thus
sometimes thrown into duress, and kept there
until the capture or death of the offender. This
measure did more to break up the system than
any other means employed for the purpose.

In addition to all this machinery for restoring
social order to Corsica, the Government constantly employed during many years a large force of
gendarmerie to ferret out the brigands. Many
daring exploits, many hair-breadth escapes, characterized this mountain warfare; and sometimes,
too, a certain chivalry was displayed, which gave
a tinge of romance to a conflict little known out
of the narrow limits to which it was confined.
But the efforts of the Government have been
crowned with success at last. The highways and
by-paths of Corsica are as safe as any in Europe;
and, although it will be ages before the vindic-
tiveness of the hot-blooded islanders shall be altogether eradicated, any one who lives in an orderly

manner, minds his own business, and controls his passions, can now live in Corsica unmolested, and die in his bed like a Christian.

Considered as a resort for tourists, Corsica offers itself as one of the most romantic and variously attractive spots in the Mediterranean ; and that is saying a great deal, as any one who is familiar with that sea very well knows. The mountains abound with game, including such lively sport as wild boars. For the artist the grandeur and beauty of the scenery are highly inspiring. The sublimity of the precipices and snow-clad peaks is unsurpassed by any other landscapes on the shores of the Mediterranean, and Nature, ever prolific with her charms in the Italian seas, has lavished the splendors of her coloring in the tints with which she has clothed this magnificent island. The ports, guarded by the ruddy pepper-box turrets and crenellated ramparts of the middle ages, rising by sands fringed with gayly painted feluccas and bare-legged fisher-folk, ever present us with satisfying objects of contemplation ; while the purple mountains, springing from the sea, soar in the background against the dome of blue, and the green azure of the Mediterranean, fading into purple in the offing, incloses the landscape with an indescribable sense of repose.

The vast chestnut-forests of Corsica are scarcely equaled by any other vegetable phenomenon of Europe for impressive beauty, and fairly rival those of Madeira. Together with the tender gray of the olive-groves, they soften the asperity of a scenery that would otherwise be sometimes almost too stern and savage to win our affections, while it might command our respect.

As regards climate, Corsica can scarcely be recommended for either the sick or the well during the summer, because of the malaria which prevails in too many quarters at that season. But from October to May this objection does not exist, and then the invalid may derive benefit from a residence in Corsica.

It is to the western coast, however, that the stranger will devote most of his time, for the low mountains and alluvial plains of the eastern seaboard, from Bonifacio to Bastia, are but thinly peopled, and the scenery is inferior to that of the other side of the island. Bastia is the chief commercial port of Corsica, and will doubtless long continue so, owing to the advantages offered by its small but secure anchorage and its nearness to the continent. In good weather steamers make the passage between Bastia and Leghorn in six or seven hours. A few hours' ride from this town, on the central ridge of Cape Corso, and near to Pino, are the remains of the tower where Seneca the Philosopher passed his exile when banished hither from Rome. His philosophy was entirely of that sort which one may hold in theory but not in practice ; and therefore this sage accepted the decrees of Fate with impatience, and railed most vigorously against the savage people and country of Corsica. Nature as such had but very few charms for the ancients ; but it is easily comprehensible that Seneca could find little to entertain him in that island, when we consider that it is only in recent years that it has emerged from its semi-barbarous condition.

But the place where, in all Corsica, the stranger can doubtless find himself best situated for the winter, both for climate and lodging, is Ajaccio, the birthplace of Bonaparte, whose house is still shown, together with its old furniture. Of late years this choice little city of some fifteen thousand souls has became a resort for numerous English and German tourists searching for a winter sanitarium, and with abundant reason. The hotel-keepers are gradually learning to appreciate the possibilities of Ajaccio as a resort, and a steady improvement is evident in the quality of their accommodations, while a number of cozy villas are ready to lease for the season on moderate terms. The society is also good, and the promenades about the town are rendered agreeable by noble avenues of plane-trees.

The Bay of Ajaccio is one of the most charming and poetically beautiful spots among many which enchant the eye and captivate the fancy. It is indeed a noble prospect that greets one as

he walks the quay of Ajaccio, and gazes over the
imperial blue of the sea, looking southward.
Around him are lemon and orange groves, and
the circular sweep of the bay is inclosed by the
majestic range of mountains which form the citadel of Corsica. Well may one exclaim in his
enthusiasm, What place more fitting to be the
birthplace of him who carried the eagles of
France from the Pyramids to Moscow? Yonder
mountains nursed in his soul the mighty and
energetic thought, and the endless expanses of
the sea fired him with a restless longing to find
scope for the expansion of his Titanic powers.

But these grand, gray mountains, that seem
to hedge Ajaccio landward and crowd it down to
the water's edge, also serve the useful purpose of
shielding it from the piercing winds of the north.
And thus we find that, to the amenity of its
scenery, Ajaccio adds the highly important advantage of being a valuable sanitarium for invalids during the winter season. The mildness
of the temperature is rendered yet more equable
by the prevalence of gentle but regular sea-
breezes, that blow almost with the steadiness of
a trade-wind.

There are many delightful excursions that
may be made from Ajaccio by diligence or private carriage over the winding roads that creep
up the sides of the precipices. One is alternately
overwhelmed by the grandeur of the scenery or

charmed by the idyllic loveliness of the green nooks steeped in quietude that burst upon him unawares.

One of the most interesting of these trips is to the valley of Liamone. Zigzagging up the scars of a curtain of granite until we are over two thousand feet above the sea, we look down into a paradise many hundred feet below, lapped in repose and seemingly shut out from a restless and troublous world by stupendous cliffs or forest-clad slopes, that environ and embrace it on three sides, while on the west the blue Mediterranean tenderly laves the yellow sands of the shore.

Nor is the seclusion of this valley wholly in appearance, for on inquiry we learn that the smiling village of Carghese, on a promontory jutting into the sea, actually contains a community which in language, customs, dress, and religion is as distinct from the rest of the population of Corsica as if it were five hundred miles away. The explanation is a curious one. Five hundred years ago, when the Turks were sweeping over the Levant, ravaging and capturing the lands of the Cross, a band of Greeks, flying from the sword of the invader, sailed westward in search of an asylum, like the Spaniards who fled in the eighth century from the Moors with St. Brandon, and, according to the legend, founded a colony in one of the Atlantic isles. These Greek fugitives came at last to Corsica, and were permitted to land.

The valley of Liamone was assigned to them, and there they have remained to this day, never intermarrying with the Corsicans, and preserving the spirit and traditions of the classic land from which their ancestors fled five centuries ago.

Another most delightful excursion can be made to the delicious valley and village of Santa Lucia di Tallano, south of Ajaccio, secluded among the mountains, over fifteen hundred feet above the sea. The famous mineral baths of Orezza, in the so-called chestnut country south of Bastia, afford another resort, charming not only for its scenery, but for the exceptional coolness of the temperature during the summer, which rarely ranges above 70°. One of the springs is chalybeate, while another is strongly impregnated with iron and sulphur. They are beneficial to those who suffer from malarial fever or cutaneous maladies. But the advantages of Corsica to the invalid are chiefly climatic. Those who are in need of mineral waters are better accommodated at the better known mineral resorts of the neighboring continent.

In this outline sketch of Corsica I have only indicated in a general manner a few of the attractions and advantages of an earthly paradise that is destined to become one of the most notable sanitariums and pleasure resorts of Europe. Those who would realize something of the old-time gamy flavor which still attaches to it, the raciness of customs fast yielding to an encroaching civilization, and the wild grandeur and solitude of primeval forests, should not delay until eyery rock and valley swarms with tourists armed with note-books and umbrellas, and brandishing Cook's tickets in every hamlet.

It is almost with regret that the lover of nature adds that the facilities for reaching Corsica are constantly increasing. It is but six hours' sail between Leghorn and Bastia, and numerous steamers ply between France, Italy, and Corsica.

MENTONE.

From the cliffs of Corsica one can see across the water the mountains which encircle the most noted sanitarium of southern Europe. The Gulf of Genoa forms a deep parabolic curve, whose northwestern side includes between Nice and Bordighera a district completely sheltered by two lines of mountains from the blasts of the north and west, which seem to have been created to shorten the life of man and prevent him from outliving the allotted span of existence, so invariably is he forced to fly from them and seek a shelter when the chronic maladies which war against humanity seize men within their relentless grip. Attacked by disease reënforced by its ally the north wind, the victim seeks hither and thither for safety, and in search of health wanders to and fro over the face of the earth.

Steamship and railway companies and the keepers of hotels thrive as a result, and thus some benefit incidentally follows from the ills to which flesh is heir. In the course of time a system may be tabulated by which every invalid may find out exactly the spot that suits his particular malady, and, going at once to this agency, will be able by a skillful plan of exchange to arrange his affairs so that he may permanently settle in some noted health resort, and there conduct his business without disturbance, even if ten thousand miles away from home. Thus each may find by unerring data the paradise especially suited to his own necessities. One line of steamers may be advertised as bound to the cure of bronchial difficulties; others to sanitaria for hypochondriacs; others for nerve resorts, and the like. Patients may apply at a grand general office supplied with minute formulas and attended by physicians skilled in making correct diagnoses. All that the invalid will have to do will be to pack his luggage and go to this central agency. Although he does not yet know what resort he is to go to, he knows that the place is waiting for him somewhere. Therefore he bids his friends a cheerful adieu, confident in the restorative qualities of the paradise to which he will be assigned by the consulting physician of the Grand Central Invalid Dispatch Company, Limited.

"You say your troubles are of a nervous turn," says the consulting physician ; "you are wakeful ; you find that you can not dance as long as former-ly without subsequent irritability ; that you can not bear the same quantity of old port you took in youth ; that the crying of a baby in the middle of the night produces a profound irritation of the system ; that the persistent visits of creditors with bills that you can not pay cause such a disturb-ance as even to affect the moral nature to the point of using emphatic language ; that even the every-day sight of your wife coquetting with gay colonels, when she thinks you are quietly smoking your pipe in the corner, has become a source of nervous annoyance that does not yield to the sub-cutaneous injection of heroic doses of morphine, and increases the action of the heart to a degree alarming both to yourself and to the welfare of the esteemed partner of your bosom. Ahem ! My dear sir, I do not wish unnecessarily to alarm you; indeed, I see nothing in your symptoms which is not capable of alleviation, and probably of cure, if you give yourself without reserve to the rem-edy now well known to suit cases like yours. Be calm, my dear sir, for I am about to recommend you to a resort so charming and efficacious that I almost wish I could have as good an excuse as you have for going there myself for several years. I

am quite sure you will agree with me that the
quiet seclusion of Pitcairn's Island will suit your
case to a dot. You go by the Isthmus of Panama,
and I would most earnestly recommend you to
give it a faithful trial, remaining there, if necessary, until all the predisposing causes are removed.
We doctors, you know, are so often blamed for
imperfect cures when the blame really lies with
the patient, who does not more than half carry
out our advice."

So advises the consulting physician ; and, as
the patient moves away to purchase a through
ticket for Pitcairn's Island, he taps the bell and
orders the attendant to usher in the next visitor.

In default of any such convenient system as
the one suggested, the invalid now too often de-
lays going to these health resorts until it is too
late, or wanders aimlessly from one to the other,
with little intelligent knowledge of the merits of
any of them, hoping to stumble, before he dies,
on some choice spot where he may haply prolong
his days.

Among the health paradises that are now
most prominently enjoying the public favor, and
are destined to hold it for ages to come, is Mentone, which is the central town and health resort
of the sanitary region on the westerly side of the
Gulf of Genoa. Mentone is to the Mediterranean
what Madeira is to the Atlantic, the culminating
point where the advantages desirable in a sanita-

rium are found more completely united than in any other spot of the Mediterranean basin.

Madeira owes its glorious climate to latitude and trade winds ; Mentone owes its rank to shelter from the winds. Its situation is exceptional, for it combines protection from keen winds with the temperature of a latitude sufficiently southerly to give force to the sun-rays.

The Gulf of Genoa makes a deep concave curve toward the north ; it is evident that this would tend at once to protect the adjacent coast from all but a southerly exposure if a friendly wall could be erected a few miles back, high enough to ward off cold winds from west to east round by the north. Now, this is exactly what we find to be the case at the Riviera or coast under-cliff of the Gulf of Genoa.

The Alps, like a bow, stretch from Nice to the Adriatic, inclosing Piedmont and Lombardy. Along the coast-line this great arc is subtended by the Apennines, skirting the Gulf of Genoa within a very few miles of the sea, and sometimes sending forth mighty spurs and buttresses which actually abut on the water. The narrow strip called the Riviera, bounded on the northwest to northeast side by the Apennines and on the other by the Mediterranean, is thus protected as if by a screen from the blasts of the north, and is fanned directly only by mild southerly sea-breezes. The protection afforded by these sheltering mountains

is yet further assured by the higher chain of the
Alps beyond, which serve to break to a degree
the force of the tempests rushing down from the
north.   The savage, piercingly penetrating northwest wind of the south of France is especially to
be dreaded by invalids.   Until I had felt it in
summer, I was unable to realize with what a terrific chill and fury the winds are capable of blow-
ing for several days in succession over the land ;
of course at sea there is nothing remarkable in
such a phenomenon.   But so effectually does the
mountain-screen inclose Mentone that even the
mistral is scarcely felt in that serene and secure
elysium.

In the flora of the Riviera, and particularly
of Mentone, we are again reminded of Madeira.
The aloe, palm, banana, lemon, oleander, and Nor-
folk pine flourish there, and the rose-colored masses of the *Bougainvillea*, which so often thrill the
heart with an astonishing luxuriance of color in
the paradise of the Atlantic, also gladden the eye
at Mentone.   On the steep, lofty road to Genoa,
near the picturesque old Moorish castle and village of Grimaldi, where the cliffs soar seven hundred feet above the sea, there is a view of the coast,
with Mentone in the middle distance, which suggests by its lines and colors the inimitable grandeur and loveliness of the prospect near Cabo
Garjao in Madeira, looking toward Funchal.   It
must be conceded, however, that the greater ab-

ruptness of the lines of the landscape of the latter makes it the more remarkable of the two. On the other hand, in furnishing facilities for excursions by carriage, the Riviera is superior to Madeira, although for short trips most visitors, especially invalids, prefer the sure-footed and docile donkeys of the neighborhood, tended by lithe, handsome girls instead of donkey-boys.

Nice and Monaco, within a few miles of Mentone, the latter only a few minutes distant by rail, have so long been known as fashionable resorts that to many the whole district is associated with gayety and pleasure, and is regarded as a center for gamblers and questionable characters rather than a sanitarium for invalids. This is true to a certain extent, especially with Monaco. Intrenched as on a citadel, fashionable gambling holds sway in the rocky little peninsula on which Monaco is built ; while Nice, agreeable as it is, is yet too near the outer edge of the pale of protection furnished by the coast mountains to be a resort for invalids so much as for wealth- and pleasure-hunters. It is the little town straggling on one side up the talus of the mountains, and on the other reaching out over the sea on a promontory terminating in an old Genoese castle, that furnishes the invalid the finest winter retreat of the Mediterranean, Mentone by the sea.

For ages the little town nestled there, scarcely known. The hardy peasants toiled century after

7

century, and with infinite patience terraced the
steep slopes of the hills and ravines, and planted
the groves of olive, orange, and lemon, the vineyards and shade-trees, which give such beauty to
the place and win for it the affections of all who
make its acquaintance. In those days of the long
ago the sturdy lords of yonder ruined castle on
the upland cliff levied black-mail from passing pilgrims and merchants, and the white sails of the
Saracen and Algerine corsairs were seen stealing
like swallow-wings over the dreamy blue of the
Mediterranean, which, impartial as the sunshine of
heaven, has served to bear the good and the evil
alike to their destinations. Although ever on the
alert, the people could not always prevent the descents of the pirates, nor always escape the far-
reaching clutches of the Moor, which, like the long
tentacles of the devil-fish, stretched across the
Mediterranean to the coast of Italy, and drew
thence the screaming maiden, torn from her mother's arms, with streaming hair and eyes raining
tears, to bewail her fate in the wife-market or
behind the harem-lattice of Constantinople or Al-
giers.

What a world is this! Without sorrow and
blood, without tragedies unnumbered and unutterable, where would be the romance that gilds
the pages of history and gives such a boundless
interest to the ever-living story of humanity?
Without the crimes and cruelty and hardness of

men, where would be the tragic muse of Sopho-
cles, the immortality of Shakespeare, the thrilling
lamentations of Clarissa Harlowe, the mysterious
agonies of Hester Prynne? Take away the iron
rule of the feudal lords of the middle ages, the
remorseless wars of Christian and Saracen, and
all the other terrible deeds of the past, and Italy
would be as tame in the great element of human
interest as the primeval forests of America.

What then? Are these convulsions and
crimes foreseen and intended by a great law that
thus gives muscular force to the character of nations, and at the same time out of the sufferings
of one generation affords the men of the next
material for stimulating their sympathies, their
imagination, and their arts? Is all seeming evil
only benefit in disguise? Is all energy developed
somewhere, somehow, some time into use for the
race? Are the moral forces like the physical
forces of nature, even when most fierce and apparently uncontrollable, working upon certain
lines of law? Those who most vehemently deny
the possibility of the truth of these observations
are, however, utterly unable to prove the reverse.
We know so little, we are surrounded by and
move in such an impenetrable cloud of mystery,
that no one can with any certainty assert that he
has got at the truth of these matters. This much
is certain, however, that even the best, the most
pure-minded, the most tender-hearted, can not

avoid acknowledging a deeper attraction in those
spots in which natural and human or historical
interest are combined. A landscape, however
magnificent and sufficient in itself, receives yet
another and perhaps deeper charm when invested
with human associations, even when they are
tinged with tragedy and crime.

And thus we confess that the Riviera of Genoa
is rendered yet more enchanting by the historic
halo that glorifies it, and that as we ride among
the steep, winding lanes round about Mentone,
the gentle stimulus ever afforded to the imagination by the traces of the men of other days, adds
to the transports with which the cultivated mind
gazes on the glorious prospects revealed at every
turn.

And thus the ages came and went. War's
wild tempest swept over Europe, empires arose
and fell, and Mentone, at the foot of the mountains, by its own little sheltered bay, with its own
tragedies and festal days, its own funerals and
marriage bells, lay there by the sea, unknown
to the world at large. But its destiny, though
long in coming, was yet no less sure; and it
came.

I well remember the delight I experienced
when I first read in college Ruffini's beautiful
romance entitled " Dr. Antonio." His glowing,
enthusiastic descriptions of the Riviera first attracted my attention to a spot which in a few

years was destined to become yet more famous as one of the two choicest sanitariums yet discovered for invalids. It is to Dr. Bennett, an able English physician, who was himself in search of a spot suited to his own complaint and easily accessible by land, that the world is indebted for the discovery of the advantages offered to invalids by Mentone.

We now know, as so many have proved, that invalids who seek both a mild and a dry temperature can find it at Mentone. A moist heat, as every one knows, is debilitating rather than beneficial. In houses with a southern exposure the glass rarely falls below 56° at this enchanting spot, and thus one can sleep with open windows and be ever sure of pure oxygen. At Mentone the mortality from consumption in cases of invalids is scarcely one in fifty-five ; in England it is one in five, and in Massachusetts one in three.

San Remo, a few miles eastward from Mentone, is also becoming a climatic resort, having gained popularity in this respect within a few years. Similar in climate, it is possibly less picturesque, but it is well provided with good accommodations for invalids, and is only four miles from Bordighera ; it is the scene of Ruffini's romantic novel, " Dr. Antonio," and is also noted for the finest palm-grove in Europe. Indeed, it is doubtful whether this tropical plant could grow elsewhere on the Continent as it does in the Riviera. It is to those groves that the Papacy has long looked for palm-branches to celebrate Palm Sunday in Rome.

It should be added that it is hardly expedient for invalids to pass the summer at Mentone. The season for them is really between October and May; after that the invalid can receive more benefit by going to the Channel Islands or the Valley of Orotava.

THE SOUTH OF FRANCE.

MOVING westward from the Riviera of Genoa, ever searching for that variety which is said by philosophers to be the condiment of life, the wanderer in search of health and happiness finds in the South of France a land which pleases the eye and the fancy alike, seduces the senses and invigorates the intellect. Here, between the Gulf of Lyons and the Bay of Biscay, are two paradises divided by the sere waste lands of the Corbières : the paradise of Provence, of which Avignon is the center, watered by the Rhône and dominated by the grand and lovely peak of Mont Ventoux, and the paradise of the Pyrenees, of which Pau is the center, guarded by the awful Pic du Midi. I know of no part of Europe where a lovely scenery and a delightful climate have been more effectively aided by a wealth of historic antiquities and the indescribable charm of great historic associations, except Attica ; and there we do not so much find a luxuriance of vegetation as a suggestive and glorious combination of tone and color.

Avignon, on the banks of the Rhône, is girt by a coronal of mediæval towers united by the battlements of picturesque walls. These fortifications give us one of the finest illustrations now existing of the strong-walled towns of the middle ages ; they completely surround the city, and have been thoroughly restored by the celebrated architect Viollet Le Duc. In the heart of the city stands the enormous palace of the Popes, who, it will be remembered, reigned at Avignon during the fourteenth century. The vast towers which surmounted this edifice have been shorn away by modern vandalism, but the main structure still remains, one of the grandest and most sumptuous monuments of the gay, turbulent, romantic period which it commemorates. Those were indeed days of festivity and of blood—the troubadour sighing under his lady-love's window his nightingale song, while in the neighboring dungeon the rack of the Inquisition tore apart the muscles of its victim. In his banqueting hall the Pope drank deep out of his golden beaker, while in the cell underground Rienzi, the noblest man of his age, shut out from the sunlight and the stars, felt the chains gnaw at his bones.

The exterior of this palace is of a most grim and tremendous aspect, and the effect is not lessened by the machicolations or apertures under the overhanging ramparts through which in time of war the besieged poured boiling pitch and melted lead upon the heads of the assaulting columns below.

On entering the building we are therefore not surprised to find long, winding, and gloomy stairways and corridors inclosed by walls of enormous massiveness, that strike awe to the heart, as if they led to some mysterious halls of oblivion, as in some cases they do. The *oubliettes* of this fortress palace are actually two stories below the foundation, where the rays of the sun have never penetrated. But after visiting them it is a striking contrast to ascend to the halls where the Pope and his vast retinue of servitors dwelt in the utmost magnificence of which the middle ages were capable.

Of late years the building has been occupied as a barrack, and the gilded frescoes of the vaulted ceilings have been whitewashed in a most ruthless manner. Nevertheless, one can partially discern in the carved stonework what must have been the splendor of the Pope's audience chamber in the days when Petrarch and Laura passed through those halls, and Rienzi made his appeal to John XXII. But, when I was there, a company of infantry was quartered in this very apartment. When we reached the center of the room the garrulous *Provençale*, who was showing me around the building, stopped to give me an elaborate account of the palace. Some of the soldiers who were cleaning their arms clustered around us to listen to the conversation. Suddenly, with a quick jerk of the head, she said to me, "What are you? Are you an Englishman?"

"No," said I.

"Well, then, you are not a Frenchman, are you?"

"No, I'm not a Frenchman."

"Well," and she looked at me almost fiercely, while the soldiers stepped closer as if keenly interested in my reply, "it can't be possible that you are a German?"

"Well, and what if I am?" I replied, looking at her with simulated defiance. A moment of breathless silence succeeded, and then I said quietly, "But I am not a German. I am an American."

"Ah, that is much better," the woman exclaimed, while they all gave such a sigh of evident relief that I was tempted to laugh in their faces.

A few steps from the palace of the popes is the Cathedral of Notre Dame, an unpretending Romanesque structure overlooking the city. The portico is an elegant specimen of early Christian architecture ; the interior is simple, massive, and entirely devoid of all signs of Gothic styles. To

the student of archæology it is a very interesting
building, but to the poet or sentimentalist it offers
especial attractions as the church of Petrarch and
Laura. In one of the chapels is the exquisitely
beautiful tomb of John XXII. The types of
Provençal beauty which one meets among the
worshipers serve at once to warm the fancy and
to carry one back to the olden days of romance
and song.

One hot noontime I sought shelter in the cool
aisles of the cathedral. Passing as I did from
glare to gloom, my vision was at first confused,
and I supposed that I was alone in the building;
but as I became accustomed to the twilight, I per-
ceived an elderly woman approaching me, accompanied by a young girl. I accosted them, and
inquired for the sacristan, but scarcely heeded
their reply, I was so astonished by the picture before me. The maiden, with her hands crossed on
her breast, her eyes uplifted, and her lips still vi-
brating as if with the prayers she had scarcely
finished repeating, and an almost seraphic ecstasy
in her pure and innocent features, appeared exactly as if she were one of Fra Angelico's angels
stepped out of the canvas. It was one of those
bits of real life that one meets at long intervals, which seem invested with the garb of the
ideal.

But I saw another scene that evening which
brought me back to the hard realities of life be-

low. Crossing the Rhône on the suspension bridge toward sunset, I stationed myself where I could see on the one hand the ever-shifting and passing train of peasantry, some returning to the villages from market, and others going back to town after a hard day in the fields. The towers beyond carried the mind back to other days, but the men and women that I saw were bending and reeking with the toil of the nineteenth century. The prose and the poetry of life were there, but they did not seem to be in full accord ; therefore I turned and gazed restfully on the faint purple outline of Mont Ventoux, delicately penciled against the opalescent tints of the sky like the shadow of a vast pyramid. In the foreground rushed the blue arrowy current of the Rhône, on the one bank the city, on the other the old castellated suburb of Ville-Neuve-lès-Avignon ; between the two the broken remains of the bridge of St. Bénézet, said to have been constructed by a pious youth of that name in the dark ages, who was most likely a clever young architect, sainted after he acquired reputation. While I was thus gazing alternately at scenery and people, a care-worn, middle-aged man in a blouse came down to the bank of the river and laid aside his habit ; then, before any one could divine his purpose, he jumped into the rushing river, which was shooting by like a mill-race. There was no boat within half a mile of the spot. To try to save him by jumping in after him would be to court his fate. The whirlpools carried him to the center of the stream ; a few short moments he floated, and then sank out of sight.

That was enough of tragedy for one day. Recrossing the bridge and threading the narrow lanes of Avignon, I climbed to the public garden behind the cathedral, lit my cigarette, and called for coffee ; but I enjoyed them not on that evening with the repose of mind which they are expected to impart.

The precipitous rock which rises abruptly behind the city above the Rhône has been laid out in a promenade, that commands a vast prospect over the affluent beauty of Provence. In the north Mont Ventoux looms majestically against the sky, above an undulating plain well watered, dotted with towns, villas, and ruined feudal towers— a landscape of extraordinary magnificence. Around the foot of the precipice rushes the deep but rapid current of the Rhône.

An attendant brings us coffee and tobacco, and in the shadow of softly moaning pines we listen to the chiming of the bells from the city below, until the rapt fancy bears us away from the present into those ages when Roman and Gaul, Saracen and Crusader, knight and troubadour, alternately moved over yonder plains, alternately held sway, and passed away. If Provence has a fault in her charms, it is that the historic

element, the associations of human interest, are so
great as well-nigh to overpower the influence of
nature, and thus prevent the scenery and the life
of to-day from exerting over the senses that all-
sufficient interest which should be the main attraction of a paradise where we seek peace for
the mind and soothing influences for the senses.

In the paradise of Béarn this element less
occupies our attention. It is true that the remi-
niscences of chivalry are everywhere about us,
while the château of the house of Navarre at Pau
constantly recalls the romantic life and character
of that gaillard and well-beloved king, Henri IV.,
for there he was born and reared ; his cradle is
shown there to this day ; and some of the most
sumptuous halls of the middle ages, replete with
stories of romance and tragedy, are within that
most interesting palace of olden time. But, after
all, Nature asserts herself here, and is the ever-
present attraction, to which she adds a most seductive climate, that renders this a health resort
for the invalid when other lands are frozen or
thrashed with sleet and rain. Thermal springs
possessing various healing qualities also abound,
and they must indeed be forlorn who can not find
in Béarn health, solace, and repose. I was at first
at a loss to account for the different force of the
influence of nature in Provence and Béarn, since
the scenery of each seems equally lovely. But
I came at last to think that it is the mountains

which give such a predominating power to nature
in the latter region. A grand range of mountains
is like an individual of decided character ; it dar-
ingly asserts itself, and allows no other feature of
the scenery to take from it the ascendancy. Thus
the stupendous peaks and gorges of the Pyrenees
are present in every Béarnese landscape, now ad-
vancing with mighty shoulders into the verdure
of the plains, and anon retiring to the end of a
long winding valley, whose idyllic beauty is musical with the prattle of streams. And, however
savage the serrated outline of the Pyrenees, and
however stern they are when we penetrate to their
inmost recesses, their general aspect on the northern face is cheerful ; for they are clad with forests and seem to catch something of the joyous
character of the Béarnese themselves, while not
altogether relaxing from the character they feel
bound to assume as large mountains. In midwinter, whitened with deep snows, their appearance is Alpine.

Who that has sat and dreamed under the grand
colonnades of trees on the esplanade of Pau can
ever forget that magnificent scene ? The old city's
peaked and mossy roofs cluster one above another
on a steep declivity overlooking a vast plain, whose
ample verdure is intersected by the foaming waters
of the Gave d'Ossau ; and the picture is inclosed
by the purple ranges of the Pyrenees, above
whose center, in a cleft of the mountains, rises

the sublime obelisk of the Pic du Midi, regular as if sculptured by the giants of primeval ages.

At that distance the Pyrenees look like a wall, scarcely suggesting the depth of their ravines and valleys. But if you take a coach and ride toward the Pic du Midi up the Val d'Ossau, you shall traverse nearly twenty-five miles before you even begin to ascend the mountains. Of all the exquisite valleys of the Pyrenees, not even excepting the charming vale of Lourdes, none seems to me to exceed this Val d'Ossau for poetic loveliness. Everywhere, a silver serpent stealing among the vineyards and orchards, now silent and anon chattering blithe music, the Gave glides across the roadway. Meadows lush with harvests and flowers, and picturesque with vine-hung poplars or willows, stretch away to the green precipices which on either hand inclose this enchanted valley. The song of the peasant falls pleasantly on the quietude of the summer's day. At intervals of three or four miles we come to hamlets by the river-side, where, of course, the postilion must have his chat with Marguerite or Ninon while they are changing the horses, and doubtless wins at least a glass of eau-de-vie if not a stolen kiss or two. There is an epicurean atmosphere about everything, that makes one look leniently and perhaps enviously at the varlet, who, having mounted the box, now cracks his long lash in a scientific and artistic style that produces the double result of starting the four horses away at a tearing gallop and filling the bystanders of both sexes with admiration and delight. It is not until we arrive at Laruns, a most entertaining and picturesque hamlet, that we fairly reach the heart of the Pyrenees, and begin to storm the stupendous bastions that loom above us far up in the clouds, sublime and terrible as if begotten by the glacier and the thunderbolt.

NORTH OF PORTUGAL.

It is not a long journey from Pau to Portugal. Of all the travelers who visit the continent for health or pleasure, how few ever go to Portugal, and thus how few know that it is the most beautiful country in Europe. I am aware of no region on the mainland that, within so limited a space, offers such a variety of scenery. In the south is a parched region, for all the world like a bit of the opposite coast of Barbary, of which it very likely formed a part at some remote period. Adjoining this is a district of plain that would be monotonous if it were not everywhere carpeted with a profusion of rank vegetation, so rich and varied in color as to suggest an elaborate pattern of Persian embroidery. Lisbon itself possesses a port and bay scarcely inferior in beauty to Na-

ples ; and the neighboring heights and town of
Cintra combine in a most enchanting and extraordinary manner the charms of sea and precipice,
palace and garden.

The central portions of Portugal are in turn
savagely romantic and mountainous, haunted by
the boar and the wolf ; while the delights of the
scenery of Coimbra and the Mondego, and the
legends which cling to their feudal walls, fascinate the cultivated imagination. But, as if this
were not enough, this choice little kingdom offers
us yet greater attractions. When you have sated
your appetite on the rest of Portugal, then go to
Oporto, and from the tremendous gorges of the
Douro enter the paradise of the Minho e Douro,
a province small in size, but exceeding in beauty
any spot I have seen in Europe. First tarry a
few days at Oporto, for it is gloriously situated,
and is the great shipping center of the port wine
trade.

Port wine, *par excellence*, is all made in the
district of the Alto Douro, in the southern part of
the province of Tras os Montes, along the banks of
the Douro, down which the wine is eventually
brought in boats to Oporto. The average yield
is fifty thousand pipes, of which thirty-five thousand are exported to England, and the business is
entirely controlled by the English. Old port, in
Oporto, is something similar to nectar of the gods ;
few are the privileged mortals who ever taste any-

thing equal to it beyond the confines of Portugal.
To be really worth drinking, it must mellow at
least ten or twelve years in the dark lodges or
vaults at Gaia, opposite Oporto, where immense
quantities of this "liquid sunshine" are stored.
As it grows old, it assumes a tint suggesting alternately ruby and molten gold, as the light happens
to strike it.

The situation of Oporto is superb, at the opening of a gorge, on an excessively steep acclivity,
and so divided by a ravine as to offer some very
effective massing of light and shade, together
with delicate tints at sunrise and sunset.   There
is a lack of spires in the outline, but the want is
partially obviated by the magnificent tower of the
Eggrego dos Clerigos, on the highest point of the
southern portion of the city, sustaining its gilded
cross nearly six hundred feet above the river. On
the abrupt, pinnacle-like hill at the northern end
of the city the towers of the cathedral and the
bishop's palace, although in themselves not remarkable, contribute by their position to that
general effect which makes Oporto from a distance one of the finest cities in Europe.

Many of the streets are wide, although very
steep, and the houses well built, and exceedingly
neat, with their facing of *azulejos* or glazed figured
tiles.   The people are generally spirited and good-
looking, but inclined to express discontent by re-
volts.   Strangers will be struck with the elegant

equipages common here as well as at Lisbon, and
with the reckless speed with which they are driven
down the steepest slopes. Another feature peculiar to Oporto, and worthy of imitation elsewhere,
is the place where fresh milk is sold. It is a neat
stable, into which the cows are driven each morning. In front is a counter, and when a customer
requires a quart of milk it is drawn before his
eyes ; adulteration is thus impossible, while the
condition of the cow shows that the quality of
the milk must also be pure.

At Oporto I took the diligence for Braga and
a trip through portions of the Minho district,
which has the reputation of offering some of the
most beautiful landscapes in Europe. I was not
disappointed in what I saw. The diligence started
at nine, and was drawn by six horses, three abreast,
the common mode of harnessing horses in Portugal. As usual, the luggage and a number of the
passengers were on the top. We started at full
gallop, going at a rapid rate up the long slope
leading out of the city. Crossing the Leço, we
came to Villanova, changed horses, and reached
Braga toward night. The country increased in
beauty with each mile, giving everywhere evidence of high culture. Vines were trained on
trees as well as on trellises, adding luxuriance to
the verdure ; the villages were always neat and
thrifty, and new houses were going up everywhere in the Minho, sufficient proof of the grow-

ing prosperity of the country. The landscape was very broken and the road was rarely level, sometimes winding up a long, steep ascent. Mountain-ranges were to be seen on every side.

Braga lies on a hill in the center of a noble valley; its battlements and towers were visible a long distance, through embowering foliage, before we finally dashed up its narrow streets at a furious rate, amid a lively tarantara from the bugle of the postilion and a continuous volley from the long whip of our coachman. Every diligence-driver in Portugal carries two whips, a short one for the wheel-horses, a heavy and fearful weapon, and a long lash for the leaders, which the driver cracks in a manner that may be ranked among the fine arts.

Braga is a city of great antiquity, numbering sixteen thousand inhabitants. It was founded by the Romans in 296 B. C.; afterward it became the capital of the Suevi, and later an important place in the early history of Portugal. The Archbishop of Braga disputes the primacy of the Spains with the Archbishop of Toledo, and the claim is indicated by a cross with triple bars wherever a cross can be planted, besides weather-vanes on every spire, representing cherubs holding miters, keys, crosiers, and the like; but, as most of them have lost their gilding and are black with rust, they as often look like imps as like angels.

The cathedral has a beautiful flamboyant porch

with triple arch, and the exterior of the choir or apse is also highly ornate and elegant ; but the interior has been improved and restored out of all character with the original. Braga is full of choice bits of antiquity—here an old tower, and there a mullioned window or quaint chapel. But the glory of the place is in its situation. One may allow his steps to wander at random in any direction, and he will always discover some beautiful prospect or idyllic nook. The chapel of St. John, in a vale near a brook spanned by two arched bridges close at hand, shaded by lime and cork trees, and musical with the singing of nightingales, or of girls washing their clothes, is a lovely spot morning and evening. Nostra Senhora de Guadalupe is situated in the midst of an inclosure on a knoll shaded by olive and cypress trees and stone-pines. The view in every direction is enchanting.

Two miles from Braga, on the summit of an eminence some eight hundred feet above the plain, is the church of Bom Jesus, one of the most beautiful and curious resorts in the kingdom. It is a pilgrimage shrine, and is reached by an excellent zigzag road densely shaded. But the devout pilgrim will prefer to climb the steep ascent by the elaborate stairway that leads directly to the sacred spot, and is provided at the landings with chapels. These chapels are sixteen in number, square, with conical roof, and have a grating through which is visible in each a group of life-size figures representing some scene from the life of the Saviour. These groups are colored, and are in some cases not without merit. Near the summit, the hill on each side of the stairway is most elaborately terraced, and planted with flowers and cedars. The terrace expands to a semicircular platform before the church, and is surrounded by marble statues of the more noted characters who took part in the world's great tragedy. The church is of considerable size, and has little pretension to beauty, but is, on the other hand, free from the vulgar tinsel-work which cheapens so many Roman Catholic churches in Portugal and Southern Europe.

The prospect from this terrace is one of the most remarkable in Portugal, at once lovely and sublime, commanding the silver line of the ocean, the verdure and the glory of the Minho valleys, and the grandeur of the sharply formed, purple-hued pinnacles of the Gerez. Under the lime and plane trees adjoining is the place where pilgrims bake their bread in rude ovens in the open air. The hotel of Boa Vista, the best I met outside of the capital, is a stone's throw from the church. This spot affords many pleasing walks, and may be recommended to tourists or invalids as well as to pilgrims. I like the idea of the place better than that of most religious resorts, because no saint, mythical or otherwise, is obtruded ; the shrine is dedicated to the founder of the Christian religion, and to him alone.

Having arrived at Braga, one is so well satisfied that he wants to stay arrived. He finds it is not necessary to go to the "hollow Lotus land" in order to eat lotus; it can be done at Braga. Not because the accommodations offered the traveler at the inn are sumptuous, for they are rather the reverse. Out of Lisbon, the traveler in Portugal, with a few exceptions, will find little to praise in the inns of the country. But in such a climate one lives out of doors and basks under the pines, and thus thinks less of the quality of the hotels. Then, too, the people are so generally cheerful and polite that one soon feels at ease with them. The Portuguese are a galliard and hospitable folk, affable, good-hearted, and generally mild-tempered. But they are none the less high-spirited on that account, and may not be trifled with any more than other people.

The 1st of December is always celebrated with immense enthusiasm : it is the anniversary of the day when the people, in 1640, arose and overthrew the tyranny of the Spanish dominion usurped by Philip II. after the death of Dom Sebastian at the battle of Alcazarquivir. There is no love wasted between the two peoples : the Portuguese can not forget the Spanish yoke, while the Spaniards can not forget that, from the famous battle of Aljubarrotta down to the war of independence, the Portuguese have beaten them in almost every battle, and once carried their standard into Madrid itself. It is a mistake, also, to suppose that the Portuguese language is so very inferior to the Spanish : this is, to say the least, as yet an open question. The Portuguese has many delicate modes of expressing shades of thought quite peculiar to itself, and is in construction more nearly like the ancient Latin than any of the cognate tongues. The orthography is, however, not yet quite settled ; the same word, and that, perhaps, a proper noun, may be spelled in different ways. Nearly one thousand Moorish or Arabic words are in constant use.

Nor are these the only signs of the former Saracenic dominion in Lusitania. The *cuisine* is quite Oriental : a dish of rice resembling *pilaff* is invariably the second course at dinner. The people have an Eastern relish for sweets, and excellent preserves are common when everything else, perhaps, is barely eatable. The coffee is generally good ; the tea, of which the Portuguese are very fond, is always good. The clapping of hands in lieu of the ringing of a bell is quite Oriental. It is by no means uncommon to meet men of remarkable personal beauty who are of unquestionable Morisco descent. The politeness of the Portuguese seems also borrowed in part from the Oriental, although it so often springs apparently from kindliness of nature that I am inclined to consider it an original trait of the Portuguese character. No people I have met have struck me as so unaffectedly polite, so full of unselfish courtesy in the ordinary dealings of life, so gracious and hospitable, as the Portuguese. This politeness extends from the lowest to the highest, and pervades the whole nation.

As regards other social traits, it may be said that the Portuguese lose nothing in comparison with other Latin races on the score of modesty and morals. There are certain Saxon notions of propriety which do not enter into Latin minds, and therefore should not be expected of them. The Portuguese are warm-hearted, and there seems to be considerable domestic unity and affection among them. Marriage is rather more the result of love than the mere matter of business or *convenance* that it is too often in France and Italy. It is a noteworthy fact that the Portuguese women are inferior to the men in physical beauty. The difference is more marked in the upper than in the lower classes ; perhaps the type, dark and semi-Oriental, requires the picturesque costume of the peasantry to do it the justice which it certainly does not receive from the fashions of Paris.

The masculine sex of the little kingdom displays a truly feminine weakness for dress. To cut a figure on the *pracca* of an evening in pantaloons that set off to the best advantage the nether limbs of the wearer, and to move and pose the

person with studied effect, are apparently the chief
end of being to the young coxcombs of Lisbon
and Oporto.   The gold lace sported by every one
who can possibly find an excuse to put on a uniform would almost pay the national revenue.
However, this little foible is set off by the skill
shown in managing the superb steeds which often
grace the esplanade.   The Portuguese also make
good sailors—the best of all the Latin races, as the
writer can testify from personal observation.

It is a morning's ride from Braga to Ponte da
Lima.   This is reputed by the Portuguese to be
the finest view in the kingdom, which is saying a
great deal for it.   After hearing that, although
very well content with Braga, I was of course
bound to see Ponte da Lima.   My coachman
looked like a rogue, and, from certain suspicious
stories he told about himself with much zest,
I am inclined to think that he was several re-
moves from saintship.   But the worst quality he
displayed during the ride was an endless capacity
for chattering, for which I blamed him ; to which
he added a propensity to joke with the pretty
peasant girls, for which I blamed him less.

Crossing a low, sere ridge which divided the
plain, whose beauty was so continuous as almost to
be monotonous, the valley of the river Lima suddenly unfolded itself to view.   Following a gentle
descent, we reached the town by the side of the
river.   It is more difficult to describe a screne

and quiet beauty than one that is strongly marked and forces itself at once on our enthusiasm. It is easier to paint the portrait of a rough soldier than of a fair woman, and do it well. I can only mention what seemed the characteristic features of so celebrated a view, and leave you to imagine the rest. In my memory it dwells as one of the few absolutely perfect and satisfying landscapes I have seen.

There is a little town on a slope dropping to the banks of a river. Every house is draped with ivy, and a cluster of feudal towers by the brink is almost hidden by the velvety green of the ivy that festoons their gray masonry. A little market-place near the water, and a wain creaking along the pier, give just sufficient animation to prevent the place from seeming wholly given over to slumber. A long reddish-gray bridge, supported by twenty-four Gothic arches, and venerable with half a thousand years, spans the Lima, and on the northern bank meets a group of villas, where the merry country girls come down and wash their linen, like Nausicaa when met by Ulysses. The gardens which overhang the water are closed in by a delicately outlined amphitheatre of mountains, mirrored in the still surface of the silent gliding river.

The Lima was reputed by some to be the Lethe of mythology, for which reason Lucius Brutus had great difficulty in persuading his army to cross.

Many Portuguese poets have celebrated the charms
of the Lima. Indeed, this spot is considered the
most beautiful in Portugal. As my expectations
were great, the quiet character of the landscape
at first failed wholly to realize my anticipations.
There is nothing about it to make a vivid impression at a glance. But the longer I gazed, the more
my rapture grew, until I was able to see that it is
not on any one feature that Ponte da Lima depends
for the subtle influence it weaves over the soul,
but on a happy combination of light and color,
mountain, grove, and river, hoary bridge and ivied
battlement, in a harmonious whole. As one looks
from the bridge, on either side a picture is presented so calm, so beautiful, so majestic, so satisfying, that it seems impossible for the highest art
to add to the felicitous arrangement.

I returned to Braga by way of Ponte Novo
and Palmiera. The *vendas* or wayside pot-houses,
and the *estalagems* or inns, are always known by
a bush hung over the door in the Minho e Douro,
and generally through Portugal ; hence the proverb, " Good wine needs no bush." The road was
often blocked with ox-carts of the most primitive
character, consisting of two solid wheels and a
round axle, the whole turning ; the cart rests in a
groove on the axle, and is kept in place merely by
its own weight. Nothing simpler could be devised. The cart is drawn by a band of hide attached to the horns of the oxen, sometimes to their

foreheads. The yoke, which plays quite a subordinate part, is often over a foot broad, of oak elaborately carved, and hung with tassels. Some of these yokes are very old, dating even four centuries back. The enormous horns of the oxen give a very picturesque effect to one of these rustic turn-outs, although nothing quite so foolish ever was seen as the expression of young bullocks with their prodigious appendages. The carts of Portugal are gifted with an almost incredible power of sound. This is kept in view in their construction. The sound is alternately a squeak and a groan long drawn out, and so loud that it may be heard nearly a mile on a quiet day. The chorus from a train of carts is deafening. The noise was devised, it is said, to frighten away the wolves, which are still abundant in the mountains. It is certainly hideous enough to accomplish the desired end, and would doubtless fill a legion of demons with unqualified dismay.

Four coaches started out of Braga at 6 A. M. sharp for Guimaraens, from the street of San Marcos, which, by the way, is quaint enough with its projecting stories and balconies, gaudy colors, and trumpet-like spouts. We went at a gallop much of the way, the drivers endeavoring to pass each other, although we had to climb and descend the Falaperra range. A sharp angle in the road suddenly disclosed Guimaraens, embosomed in foliage, on a gentle slope in a hollow of the moun-

tains, and crowned by a mediæval castle. This
place was the first capital of Portugal. Alfonso
Henrique was born here, and built the castle, which
is scarcely injured by "Time's effacing fingers."
The stately keep, the pointed battlements common in the fortresses of the country—all are there
as of old.

The palace first occupied by the sovereigns
of Portugal is close to the castle—a quadran-
gle in good preservation, in three sides of which
troops are quartered. The streets of Guimaraens
were the most quaint and picturesque I saw in
Portugal—narrow, with projecting eaves and balconies, and marvelous water-spouts of many fan-
tastic forms.

Having "done" Guimaraens, I took an outside passage for Oporto, *via* Santo Thyrso, one of
the most charming and delicious little rural towns
imaginable. It haunts the memory like an ode
of Keats, and, from the summit of the mountain which the road passes over a few miles beyond, a third of Portugal may be seen. The
Minho and the Beira districts lie spread out as on
a map, bounded by the Atlantic. In the extreme
north rises Gaviarra or Outiro Major, the highest
mountain in the kingdom, soaring eight thousand
feet; in the south the rugged range of the Es-
trella, which is nearly as lofty.

As we approached Oporto toward night, the
road was thronged with peasants returning home

from market in holiday attire ; the women in black felt hats over a red or blue handkerchief, often with a load on the head, and with massive earrings and breastpins—one might almost call them breastplates—of the yellow filigree gold for which Oporto is famous ; the men with red sashes, and thrumming a guitar. The coachman, a galliard blade, was able to guide his long team through the mingled masses of carts, unruly bullocks, unmanageable kids and pigs, and sparking swains and lasses, and at the same time find leisure to wind his whip within half a hair of the eyes of some gaping urchin, or drop a bit of honeyed flattery into the ear of some giggling damsel, or fling jokes or epithets, sometimes of the broadest character, at this or that swaggering gallant.

On reaching the barrier, our baggage was examined, the invariable rule in Portugal. The contents of the tin chest of one of our passengers excited considerable mirth. An orange, a pair of slippers, a night-cap, and a brandy-bottle only served to display the emptiness of a large trunk. As he was "a lean and slippered pantaloon," with red nose and eyes, who had been drinking all the way, the empty bottle evoked almost as much laughter as if it had been full.

THE AZORES.

WE have tarried long enough on the mainland; once more let us breathe the rime of the
salt sea, and behold gray cliffs and peaks looming
above the distant waves. The mariners of old,
sailing southward and westward, sought paradises in unknown isles, and often fancied they saw
enchanted groves and towers quivering in the offing. Where they looked and found not, we find;
what they hoped for, we realize. And, if Atlan-
tis and the Isle of the Seven Cities are myths, we
know of islands not less fair and more easily
reached than those.

One hundred and ten miles at sea, if you look
sharply at sunrise, you can sometimes descry a
faint blue point that seems to dance above the
waves as the ship rises and falls on the heave of
the sea; that is the extreme summit of the magnificent volcanic peak of the Azores. With a fair
wind we rapidly lift the gray cone above the circle of clouds which plays around its base, and
then we discover at its feet the magical isle of
Fayal.

"Stand by to clew up the royals!" cries the
captain as we round-to between the two islands,
which are only four miles apart, and drop anchor
in the port of Horta, the chief town of Fayal. Horta
is a small place of only five thousand inhabitants;

but to the simple people of the Azores it seems so large and important that I remember of a young girl who went from Flores to Fayal, and thence to Boston, who would not come on deck when summoned by one of her companions to look on the splendor of the metropolis of New England as they were sailing up the harbor, because, as she said, she had already seen Horta, and she knew there could be nothing else so fine in the world.

Invalids go to Fayal during the spring and summer to recuperate their failing energies. They do well; it is a choice little island, and, without carrying one's affections by storm, its genial and healthful air and the growing attractions of its scenery gain a permanent place in our memories of pleasant lands. The sleepy quiet of the streets and the undertone of the surf beating for ever-more on the beach soothe the nerves like an ano-dyne. A visit to the shady market-place in the morning before breakfast, a stroll to the seaside in the afternoon to see the merry-eyed peasants embark on their swift feluccas to return to Pico, now and then a ride on a lazy donkey followed by a garrulous boy, will half make one think he is leading an active life in Fayal; and when the sun, approaching the western ocean, suffuses the summit of the majestic cone of Pico's noble mountain with purple fire, until the lava point seems to burn like a living coal, and kindles the vapor-like clouds floating above it with rosy fires,

9

then one is thrown into a reverent mood, and can easily imagine that he is gazing on a vast altar whereon sacrifices are burning to the God of the universe.

But when Pico overpowers by the sublimity of its mien, we can turn with delightful content to the bananas and orange-groves, the fig-trees and vines, and the superb masses of oleanders, geraniums, camellias, and hortensias, which lend illimitable beauty to the valley and the river of the Flamengoz. "Oranges!" Who has not heard of and eaten the oranges of Fayal? But, unless one has eaten them there, the less he says about them the better. The oranges of Fayal and St. Michael's are like some people of sensitive natures: they lose when they forsake their native soil. The little hamlet of the Flamengoz is the most charming of the many choice spots of this magical isle, retired as it is in a ravine, and yet looking forth peacefully upon the ocean and the aspiring summit of Pico.

The fortress-like rock of Castello Branco is another charming place for an afternoon's excursion; but when one wishes entirely to seclude himself even from the sleepy activity of Horta, then let him ride up to the Caldera or crater. Fayal is really a crust of earth formed around a slumbering volcano, the rim of whose crater is about thirty-five hundred feet above the sea. The crater itself is a circle a mile in diameter, and its perpendicular sides are seventeen hundred feet deep. By looking to his steps one may descend safely to the bottom. The floor of the crater is carpeted with moss-like vegetation. In the center is a fathomless lake, and also a small cone covered with shrubs and perforated with another crater. Over the edges of the Caldera the light clouds silently gather and spill over into the abyss like noiseless waterfalls. The solitude and the silence are sublime. I certainly never experienced elsewhere such a complete sense of loneliness as when treading on the velvet-like floor of the crater of Fayal, except when shut in by a wall of midnight blackness in a lightning-riven storm at sea.

But I saw a wilder sight when I climbed the precipitous sides of Pico, seven thousand six hundred and thirteen feet above the sea, and on the minute point of its upper cone, where the stones were hot and the steam issued forth, gazed on the tremendous coils of solid lava twisted like writhing dragons in the crater below, and, beyond and under the long ranks of clouds, the isles of the Azorean Archipelago, and the infinite blue of the ocean encircling all and fading off into the sky. The ascent of Pico occupied one day by starting at three in the morning, but two days are usually allowed for the trip.

The birds have a pretty custom at these islands. I refer to the canaries, not the gulls and petrels.

Green canaries, from which the yellow ones of domestic life are only separated by the evolution of civilization, are numerous at Fayal. One may not only hear them sing on the bushes, but he may, if sufficiently hard-hearted, also have them served up choicely grilled on a platter. During the day these songsters live in Fayal, but as night comes on they take wing and return across the strait to roost at Pico. Some naturalist of curious mind should investigate the cause of this whim ; it might lead to the discovery of certain unknown climatic and physical differences between the two islands.

There is another singular difference—curious because the reason is not clearly evident, and may be owing to a similar cause : I refer to the types of the people—especially the peasantry—of Pico and Fayal ; in fact, they are all peasants on the former. Now, why is it that the women of Fayal are less fair than their sisters of Pico, who are more finely shaped, and have more attractive and intelligent features, and a more graceful mien, being sometimes possessed of almost classical beauty ? The difference is so marked as to suggest a distinct stock.

All the summer long the idler may speculate on these questions, and dream in the soft air of Fayal, and satisfy himself with the luscious fruits of the isle. But when the winds of September begin to blow, one remembers that the dampness and storms of winter render Fayal undesirable at that season.

Then, perhaps, he may go farther southward and eastward about two hundred miles, past the tremendous precipices of St. George's Island, which I have good reason to remember, for twice I narrowly escaped shipwreck there in heavy gales; past Terceira, whose city of Angra is the capital of the Azores; past St. Mary's (where Columbus landed and offered thanks when returning from his first voyage of discovery), by submarine volcanoes, by hidden reefs and beetling cliffs, until the ragged outline of the spine of St. Michael's looms above the sea. Those pinnacle-like peaks are all dormant or extinct craters; the soil of the island is the red earth that came forth untold ages ago; and from time to time the waters around are agitated not only by the terrific storms of the Atlantic, but also by steaming geysers bursting forth from submarine caldrons, and sometimes an island springing to the surface for a few days and then disappearing. And yet these terrors are more apparent than real, and St. Michael's, with its beautiful capital, its picturesque villages, its vast and magnificent plantations of oranges, its lovely vistas, romantic gorges, and enchanting climate, may justly be considered one of the fairest paradises of this world.

Although the winter winds are nearly as violent at St. Michael's as at Fayal, yet the superior

size of the island, offering greater advantages for
shelter, renders it more advantageous as a winter
resort than its sister isle. So violent are the
winds of the Azores at that season, that the
orange plantations are protected not only by high
walls, but also by a barrier of trees, generally of
the tough species called the incenso.

Ponta Delgada, the capital of St. Michael's
and the largest town of the Azores, is a handsome city of twenty-five thousand inhabitants,
and is protected from the surges of the Atlantic
by a mole and a jetty. The streets are finely
laid out, and the cathedral, ornamented with
quaint gargoyles, is a rather imposing structure.
But the market-place is the most interesting spot
in Ponta Delgada. At six o'clock in the morning it is thronged with peasantry from the plantations. The only market-wagons one sees are donkeys, if one may use the expression ; sometimes
two of them are employed, walking side by side,
and carrying two or three barrels or baskets
swinging to a pole whose ends are laid on the
backs of the animals.

Laguna, several miles to the eastward of the
capital, is a picturesque collection of villas and
peasant-huts. The nobility have some fine places
about the island, for it boasts of several counts.
To the invalid the most interesting spot in St.
Michael's is the collection of thermal chalybeate
springs called the Furnas. They are reached by

a ride of nine or ten hours from Ponta Delgada,
by gorge and glen, through the most romantic
scenery, from which the broad ocean is ever visible. These springs have long been famous for
their healing qualities ; but, were it not for the
charming climate in which they are situated, we
should hardly consider it worth while for one to
resort to them while there are so many springs of
not inferior quality more conveniently situated
on the adjoining continent.

The Azores are nine in number. Each island
has characteristics of its own, and all are worth
visiting; the westernmost of them is Flores. They
are divided into three groups, and Flores, with its
little adjacent neighbor Corvo, stands quite distant from the others. It is only nine miles long,
and is surrounded and apparently separated from
the nineteenth century by tremendous precipices,
which dip in the most uncompromising manner
into the surges below, while the central ridge of
the island is broken into volcanic peaks. But
when the heaving billows of the Atlantic swiftly
bear the boat through a narrow break in the barrier of foam-whitened lava reefs which inclose
the little port where only boats can find a shelter, and one lands on the miniature beach and
climbs up into the little town that straggles over
the edge of the cliffs, and rambles among the
vineyards and wheat-fields along the uplands, and
makes the acquaintance of the simple island-folk,

then such a consciousness of relief comes over
him, such a feeling of repose seems to steep the
senses, that he takes a long breath of rapture
and says to himself : "Here—inclosed by this
ocean and these cliffs, and secluded from the rush
of this busy age—here at last I can begin to live ;
here at last is philosophic ease ; here is tranquillity, happiness, and peace ; here Jacques might
soliloquize, here Rosalind or Orlando might make
love as pleasantly as in the grove of Arden, if seclusion and a delicate climate and a peaceful scenery are conducive to such pursuits."

The huts of the peasantry cling here and there
to the brow of the precipices, or nestle in the ravines ; and water-fowl gather in large flocks about
the lake on the uplands. The absolute impossi-
bility of walking more than nine miles in any direction, or of escaping from the island except in
a small boat, or once in a long time when a ship
touches there for provisions, tends to curb unruly
ambition and soothes the mind with a modest if
not a very elevating content.

Santa Cruz, the only town, and numbering
perhaps two thousand inhabitants, is a most fascinating little place—at least so it seemed to me.
It is not exactly beautiful, but it is full of sentiment. There is a simple pathos in the existence
of the people who there weave the web of their
simple and unknown lives, so near to Europe, and
yet so cut off by the ocean that they might al-

most as well be in the Pacific. Small as is the town, the people are yet divided into classes as if in some large metropolis. There is the moneyed class of planters, who succeed in making a little go a great way there, who live in not inelegant houses of stone, shaded by vines and fig-trees, who send their sons to Paris and Coimbra for an education ; those sons after a while return to pass intelligent but uneventful lives in their native isle. They wield their little social sway with mingled dignity and ease, nor lord it with too high a hand over the peasants who till their fields and faithfully serve them from generation to generation. Many of the peasant-girls of Flores are characterized by an unusually fine type of Latin beauty, which it is much to be regretted they lose early.

There is an old convent in Santa Cruz, inclosed by walls and overlooking the sea. To me it offered strange attractions. On the mossy tiles of the roof the long, sere grass shook and sang in the winds from the sea, while from below for ever-more floated up the deep moan of the ocean beating in the hollow caves of the isle. Many of the cells of the quaint old building were empty, for years ago the monks all left, when Dom Pedro abolished convents throughout the dominions of Portugal. But a few of the deserted cells are now occupied by some of the poor folk of the town. Among them was an old man, who many years

ago came to Flores from the continent to pursue
the craft of a jeweler, and there he passed his days
in fashioning curious Oriental-looking ear-rings
and bracelets for the peasant-women. He was
quite a genius in his way, and a philosopher as
well, and seemed content with the spot in which
he had laid his humble fortunes. But behind his
gray beard, and in the keen eyes that flashed under his shaggy eyebrows, methought I saw a lurking regret that his powers had not sought a wider
field ; or perhaps it was some disappointment of
his early life which had left its mark upon his
character, and made itself apparent in spite of
the guise of content he wore.

I left Flores with unbounded regret, and I
have often wished myself there again. Whether
it was the seclusion, the quiet, the climate, the
charming unaffected hospitality of the people—
one or all—I can not tell ; but I was singularly
attracted by what I saw there.

THE CHANNEL ISLANDS.

It is by no means essential that visitors who
resort to the Channel Islands should be invalids ;
for many, indeed, go merely for pleasure. I am
sure not a few of the gay Lotharios one sees in
the summer evenings on the quay of St. Héliers,

the chief town of Jersey, and the not unfestive damosels who there display their charms with rollicking freedom, must be there for pleasure as well as health. But if, being an invalid, one should happen in Jersey during the winter season, he may find himself wonderfully benefited by the genial air and the inviting accommodations of the abundant boarding and lodging houses, of which Bree's is one of the best. The hospitality of the people—that is, of those who are anybody—depends upon whether one has a letter of introduction from a sufficiently exalted source. One might better have never been born than go either to Jersey or Guernsey without such credentials, unless he finds sufficient company in himself.

But, aside from these insular peculiarities, which are always even more intense in her dependencies than in Great Britain itself, the good people of Jersey, and of Guernsey also, are a wonderfully handsome race (Mrs. Langtry, the reigning belle of London, is from Jersey), and are animated by many sterling qualities. Large, well formed, blue-eyed, and meeting you with a frank, half-imperious air, speaking old Norman-French as well as the English tongue, you see in them an unmixed type of a race now nearly extinct except when mingled with other blood—the hale, hardy, iron-nerved and iron-sinewed Northmen who settled in Normandy, and, led by William the Conqueror, laid Britain at their mercy on the bloody

field of Hastings. Is there not, then, a quaint
fitness in the claim of these Normans of the
Channel Islands to be the rightful rulers and
owners of Great Britain and its possessions, since
they alone represent the Normans who captured
England?

One who looks at Jersey with a sailor's eye
would naturally consider it a most cruel and forbidding spot. It is completely beset and surrounded by a network of rugged reefs, quick-
sands, and precipices. In a gale of wind, I must
confess, I have never seen a more angry and piti-
less coast than the southern coast-line of Jersey,
beaten as it is by surges of enormous height, and
absolutely white with a roaring mass of foam,
from the fierce Corbière, girt by a *chevaux de
frise* of rocks, to the treacherous entrance of the
port of St. Hélier's. But when one is once snug-
ly within the breakwater, what a change comes
over him! He defies the roughest storms, and,
like the lotus-eaters, sings to himself that he will
no longer roam, nor sigh for the far-off, dim
home-land from which he has wandered; for he
finds the air delicate and the scenery most pleasant and seductive, and life at once assumes a cheerful cast.

There are two miniature railways in Jersey;
one runs to Gorey, and the other to St. Aubin's, a
most delightful village on a bay lined with beautiful sands. This is one of the most attractive

resorts in Jersey, and, having a front to the south, is especially desirable in the winter season.

In the days of old there were pirates or gentlemen of the seas in those waters, who found the bowers and maidens of Jersey so congenial that, quite too often for the content of the islanders, they made descents on its coast which boded no good. It was to mislead the rovers by entangling them in a labyrinth of greenery, thus giving the islanders time to overtake and waylay them, that Jersey was intersected with an inextricable system of narrow-winding lanes, constantly crossing and recrossing each other, overhung by dense foliage and lined with shrubbery and hedges closely intertwined. The result, originally due to piratical incursions, is one of exceeding loveliness and a seemingly exhaustless beauty. The choicest nooks are hidden away out of sight, and one is constantly coming unawares upon an unsuspected bower, or a lane specked with sunlight sifting through the overarching leaves, while the soft warm air even in midwinter is almost heavy with the fragrance of flowers. Cottages also greet one in the same unforeseen manner, peeping, with diamond panes, ivied gables, and thatched roofs, through glimpses of the underwood.

If one sometimes half cloys with the very richness of this rural beauty, there is Mount Orgueil Castle, near the fishing-port of Gorey—a mighty and majestic pile on the east coast, stand-

ing with a royal mien upon red granite cliffs nearly three hundred feet above the sea, grim, savage,
desolate, and sublime, beaten by the surges and
the storms, and folding in its iron heart the memory of the garrisons that have kept ward and
wassail on its ramparts and in its vaulted guard-
rooms, and the sadder memory of those who have
been hurled from its battlements or hung from
them in rusty chains which still clank from the
ramparts, or have been cast into its dark *oubliettes*, or lingered in its narrow and noisome dun-
geons.

For a shilling the present inoffensive warder
will allow one to see these things, to shudder in
the narrow cell of Pym, and to rejoice, as he
wends home to his cozy fireside, and snug cur-
tains, and warm supper at the inn, that he lived
not in those rugged days. And yet, as people
then knew of nothing better, I have no doubt
they were full as happy as we are to-day. The
world may be wiser now, it may have a larger
scientific knowledge, but it is not happier. A
certain moderate average of happiness is distrib-
uted to each generation, and no more. Knowledge
may be power, but it is not necessarily happiness,
at least in this world ; and of the next we know
little enough.

The cliffs and caves of Jersey, as of all the
Channel Islands, also furnish a great attraction
to the visitor. Often of great height and very

abrupt, and sometimes splintered into such bold points as the Pinnacle at L'Etac, which springs like a lighthouse above the edge of a precipice, they kindle the imagination, while the brilliant mosses, vines, and flowers that drape their sides like gorgeous tapestry, afford an endless study to the artist and the naturalist.

Cautiously picking her way between the net-work of reefs which beset the entrance to the artificial harbor of St. Peter's Port in Guernsey, the steamer from Jersey moored alongside the pier toward nightfall on that stormy day when I made my first visit to Guernsey. As I threaded my way up the steep winding streets to my lodg-ings at the old Government House, it seemed as if I had fallen upon some fortified rock-town of the middle ages. St. Peter's Port is crowded over a slope of considerable steepness, and is divided into the old and the new town. The former lies along the port, and is faced by a spacious esplanade protected by a sea-wall. The port was originally built by Edward I. On a rock at the end of one of the piers stands Castle Cornet, a massive pile dating back, it is asserted, to the Romans, al-though much altered, of course, since then. Three hundred years ago it was greatly injured by the explosion of its powder-magazine, which was struck by lightning.

On the esplanade stands a colossal bronze statue of Prince Albert, and adjoining it is the parish church, as it is called, *par excellence*. It is one of the oldest buildings in the Channel Islands, and well deserves attention for its architectural beauty, which is after the Flamboyant-Gothic style; it is enriched by elegant stained windows. As one wanders about the steep lanes radiating from this venerable relic of the past, he is surprised to find such austere massiveness in the buildings, and such crookedness in the narrow streets, broken by a curious succession of stairways, intersected at the landings by cross-lanes. The new town extends in the rear of the old town. While in the old quarter the houses are generally built of somber granite, in the new they are as universally enlivened by a coating of tinted stucco hung with ivy. I think it would be difficult within the same space to find elsewhere so many charming streets and houses as in the new quarter of St. Peter's Port. To almost all is attached either the family name or an attractive title in English or French, as " Grove Lodge," or " Bon Repos "; and garden-plats neatly kept, or rows of ivied elms, adorn the front.

It is the pure Norman stock that we find here, still speaking Norman-French; but the dialect of Guernsey differs slightly from that of Jersey. English is also spoken by the better families. Services in the churches and proceedings in the courts and Legislature are held in French. The islands are very nearly independent of Great Britain, being permitted virtually to govern themselves, while they owe a sort of feudal allegiance to the Queen. Stranger still, each island has a government and laws of its own. These laws still savor of the rough emergencies of the middle ages, and are sometimes quite too arbitrary for the freedom of this advanced age. Notwithstanding this semi-independence, the Queen boasts no subjects more loyal than these Normans of the Channel Isles. Some of England's most distinguished soldiers and sailors came from them, and a number of noted artists, including Millais, Naftel, and Ouless.

The islanders are generally Protestants; churches and chapels abound, and outward piety at least seems to be at a premium. The superstitions of former ages are generally losing their hold. But in localities most remote from town, and among the older people, a few curious superstitions still obtain belief. On Christmas-night there are some even in St. Peter's Port who can not be induced to draw water from a well. Others dare not enter a stable at the witching hour of midnight lest they should surprise the cattle, asses, and sheep on their knees adoring the infant Saviour.

One of the first things the stranger learns on coming to these islands is the exclusiveness of the upper classes, their *hauteur* and pride, and the contempt in which tradesmen are held. On the

10

other hand, it is said that the distinction between the "sixties" and the "forties," as the two classes are termed, is wearing away.

St. Sampson's is the only other town in Guernsey after St. Peter's Port, from which it is two miles distant. The road to it passes by the sea, picturesquely varied by here and there an old martello tower or an ivy-draped fragment of a ruined castle. The church of St. Sampson's, although the oldest building in the island, having been consecrated in 1111, offers no architectural attractions. More interesting are the Vale Castle adjoining, and the Druidic remains. Long before Rollo the Norman conquered these islands, long before St. Sampson or the galleys of Julius Cæsar crossed the seas, the Celt had braved these perilous waters in his clumsy bark, and had scaled these almost inaccessible shores. In those mist-hidden ages of an unrecorded antiquity, the Druids practiced their mystic and bloody rites here, and left dolmens and cromlechs to preserve the tale of a race that might otherwise have passed away from these isles into the utter nihilism of oblivion. Many of these interesting vestiges have unfortunately been destroyed; of those which remain, one of the most important is at L'Ancresse Common, near St. Sampson's. It is composed of seven enormous slabs of which the largest weigh thirty tons; it is seventeen feet long, ten feet wide, and four and a half feet thick. When it was opened, urns, human bones, amulets, and weapons were found in it.

St. Sampson's and the adjacent portion of the little island are invested with literary interest, as several of the scenes of Victor Hugo's "Toilers of the Sea" are laid there. Although altogether a creation of the fancy, that vivid romance is enlivened by striking and truthful descriptions of the scenery and people of Guernsey.

The south side of the island is by far the most interesting part of Guernsey to the artist or scientist. The southern coast is scalloped with several beautiful bays, presenting a great variety of grotesque granitic shapes ; the cliffs sometimes rise over three hundred feet from the delicate silvery sands at their base. Dark caverns, echoing the thunder of the Atlantic surges, are hollowed into the sides of the precipices ; and rivulets, half concealed by many varieties of flowering shrubs, musically descend from the plateau above. Icart Point, Le Moulin, Huet Bay, the Gouffre, Petit Bot Bay, Gull Rock, or Pleinmont, are alternately the favorites of the enthusiastic visitor ; but the lowering, precipitous, lightning - torn and blackened crags of Pleinmont seemed to me to offer the most sublime sea-view in Guernsey, gazing over the misty wastes of the gray and lone Atlantic, and receiving the full brunt of its surges and storms.

Near the brow of Pleinmont Victor Hugo laid

the scene of some of the most startling passages
of the "Toilers of the Sea." The small stone
guard-house which he makes the smugglers' rendezvous stands there still, near the edge of the cliff.

But to the man of business the famous breed
of Guernsey cattle is of far more interest than
cliffs and romances. By some the Guernsey cow
is more esteemed than that of Alderney; it is
larger, and its ruddy color is more decided. The
cows are milked thrice daily, and the milk is
churned without skimming; a good cow should
yield one pound of butter daily. The cows are
most carefully tended, and the grass on which
they feed is enriched by vraic, a species of kelp
gathered from the reefs at low tide. The vraic-
harvests are appointed by law, one in the spring
and one in August. Peasants and fishermen turn
out in the season with boats and carts, frequently
with lanterns at all hours of the night; it is a
picturesque occupation, although attended with
some risk from the overloading of boats or frequent sudden rising of the tides, which in the
Channel Islands are of extraordinary height and
velocity. The cows are tethered when feeding;
in this way they give more milk than if glutted
with food, and while they are cropping the grass
on one side of a field, it springs up on the other.
They are not allowed to stand much in the sun.
The breed is preserved from intermixture with
other breeds by arbitrary laws.

Facing the eastern coast of Guernsey are the islands of Herm and Jethou, about three miles distant from St. Peter's Port. The former is a mile and a half long, and in some places very bold. It is chiefly valuable as a resort for sportsmen, who give custom to the hotel. Jethou lies close at hand, but is much smaller, and peopled chiefly by rabbits.

Sark is beyond these islands, about seven miles from Guernsey. In point of scenery and situation it is one of the most romantic and attractive of the Atlantic islands. The approach to the island is almost always attended with danger, and except in mild weather no boat can either land or leave, such is the savage velocity and turbulence of the raging tides, rushing in all directions around the shore with the utmost violence, and filling the caves with hollow dirges for the wretches who have so often perished on that merciless coast. Sometimes, even in summer, weeks pass without a possibility of making a landing there. In winter one must depend entirely on half-decked Sark boats of five or six tons burden. In summer a small steamer plies between Guernsey and Sark ; but, small as it is, it can not enter the miniature port, the smallest in Europe, formed by a breakwater carried across a little cove called the Creux. The interior of the island is reached from the beach only by an opening pierced through the surrounding wall of perpendicular granite.

Sark is about three miles and a half long, and is divided into Great and Little Sark. The latter is a small peninsula at the southern end, united to the main portion by a curtain of rock about two hundred yards long, called the Coupé. (How many of the names in these islands show the Norman origin of the people!) Narrowing toward the top like a wedge, it is crossed three hundred feet above the sea by a giddy path not over five feet wide, so hazardous to an unsteady eye that one person who was born and lived to old age on Little Sark never dared to cross over the Coupé. The sublime cliffs surrounding the island are festooned with highly colored lichens ; and the magnificent caves are gorgeous with beautiful submarine vegetation and numerous varieties of algæ, shell-fish, and mollusks. The massive cluster of rocks called the Autelets, the Creux du Derrible, a wonderful cavern, and D'Ixcart Bay are among the most remarkable objects of this choice little island, whose scenery has been well suggested by the water-color paintings of Paul Naftel.

The interior of Sark is alternately pastoral and picturesque, and abounds in delightful lanes and nooks of leafy underwood. The huts of the peasantry are very massively constructed, often having walls six feet thick, probably as a protection against the gales of winter. Traces of the Druids exist, and in the dark ages Sark was the haunt of corsairs, who from this impregnable stronghold darted forth on ships passing up the Channel. Later the isle was held by the French, but during the reign of Elizabeth it was taken by an English crew by means of an ingenious stratagem, and has ever since been an appanage of England. It is still governed, however, by a feudal lord called the Seigneur, who has associated with him a legislature composed of the forty landholders of the island, who naturally are not likely to relax the law of entail.

The climate of the Channel Islands is moist but mild, and varies slightly in all, although they are so near together. The average temperature of Jersey is warmer than that of Guernsey, but more damp and relaxing. Guernsey is warmer in winter, and cooler in summer. The rainfall is chiefly from October to January, and snow is rare. The climate of Guernsey is reputed to be the most equable in Europe, while the saline properties in the air, common to small islands, render the dampness less relaxing than it would be with the same temperature on a continent. The climate of Alderney and Sark is more dry than that of the neighboring isles of the group, and they are therefore resorted to by those whose systems have become enervated by too long a residence in Jersey or Guernsey.

The Channel Islands may be recommended to those suffering from lung-diseases who require to avoid raw winds or violent and sudden changes;

and they especially afford a delightful resort from April to September inclusive. Rheumatic or neuralgic patients should be more cautious in visiting the Channel Islands ; but nervous exhaustion may be overcome by a few weeks or months at Guernsey or Sark. Tourists and invalids are furnished with all needed comforts at the numerous and excellent boarding-houses and hotels.

THE ISLE OF WIGHT.

ONE can never weary of these Channel Islands ; but if he remembers that life is short, and that it will be incomplete without having seen the Isle of Wight, he will be moved by a noble discontent until he steps foot on that far-famed paradise of England.

The Isle of Wight resembles the character of an Englishman. It shows on approach a somewhat stern, reserved, and forbidding aspect, faced as it is with lofty and uncompromising cliffs. But when one has fairly made a landing and reached its heart, then he finds it full of attraction and extending a genial welcome, which is sincere and enduring. The island is an epitome of England ; we here find in miniature many of the features of the adjacent island. Do we want to visit castles and clamber over ivied ruins, there is Carisbrooke Castle at the little shire town of Newport, near the center of the island. There are few nobler ruins of the middle ages remaining to our time. The crumbling battlements are almost hidden by a profusion of ivy. The Norman keep is a grand old pile, and the historical associations are of a nature to arouse the sympathies of all ; for there King Charles I. was imprisoned, and there his daughter, the Princess Elizabeth, died.

That religious sentiment which has always been a leading trait of the serious English character also finds material for pious reflection in the cottages and graves of the Dairyman's Daughter at Arreton and little Jane the young cottager at Bradford, the pathos of whose simple lives has been so well told by Leigh Richmond in his "Short and Simple Annals of the Poor" ; while the artist and the poet may in turn be exhilarated by the charming hamlets and towns lying in valleys or clustering on the slope of the downs. There too, on the southern coast, are the stupendous precipices of Shale and Alum Bays, the one a grand gray monotony of chalk, the other glorious with its brilliantly tinted strata, evermore reverberating the thunders of the sea and filling the soul with awe ; while the savage chasms of Black Gang Chine bring to the memory a tale of many a melancholy wreck. It was with a sort of relief that I turned thence to the gay piers of Ryde and gazed on the graceful yachts idly floating on the quiet water of a summer morning before one of the most inviting watering-places in the world.

It is but an afternoon walk from Ryde to Shanklin, the sweetest village of England's fairest isle. The cottages have been dropped here and there on the rolling surface with little attempt at order —here in a trim row on the edge of a precipice that overlooks the ocean breaking at its feet, there straggling down into a hollow and nestling under the almost impenetrable shade of closely woven shrubbery. Roses clamber over the lattices in the quaint old English windows filled with diamond-shaped panes, and maidens fair as any that Gainsborough or Reynolds painted are seen behind the hedges culling flowers.

Wandering forth from the inimitable beauty of this ideal hamlet, and strolling southward, we come to the ravine and waterfall called Shanklin Chine, where Keats probably hastened his death by exposure to its influences ; for it is not only pretty, but damp and chilly, and I remember I was glad to escape thence, and on the magnificent slope above lie on the grass and gaze on the placid azure symbol of eternity, the ocean, on the glorious afternoon of a perfect summer day.

Along this shore we are in the choicest portions of the isle, where all is so charming that one is constantly reversing the opinion and enthusiasm of the previous hour, and declaring the scene actually before his eyes more delightful than those he has just gazed upon. And thus, when we come to Bonchurch, the little village under the cliff, with its ancient miniature peak-roofed chapel and memorable graves all concealed by magnificent foliage almost overhanging the sea, we are spellbound. There is only one thing that can then draw away the enraptured wanderer, who after much roving thinks he has at last found the ideal paradise, and that is to take him on his material side. He is perchance aweary with his long stroll; whisper the magical word dinner, and suggest that at the "Crab and Lobster" at Ventnor, just beyond, one can be better entertained than any other where in the "Wight." I am happy to say that one may venture on such a statement with due regard to the truth. A more comfortable bed, a choicer dinner, at an inn, may not be found in the United Kingdom. The little low-roofed stone hostel, completely draped with ivy, which first bore the name, is still attached to the larger and more modern building that has succeeded it in the public esteem.

Behind this cozy hostel soars Boniface Down, a steep cliff many hundred feet high; and below it are the roofs of Ventnor, ranged along precipitous streets and crooked lanes. The town is clustered over the famous Undercliff, whose formation can be best described by saying that several ages ago a vast piece of the Down broke away and tumbled toward the sea. A narrow, winding, undulating plateau was thus made between the cliff and the ocean, with a precipice on either side, one dipping to the beach, the other soaring from the Undercliff against the sky, seamed and bastioned and crenellated like a tremendous fortress. The plateau which forms the Undercliff is a most extraordinary and beautiful piece of irregular ground, interspersed with natural mounds that have in the course of ages become overgrown with turf and trees.

It is on this rough but exceedingly picturesque ground that Ventnor is built, and is now rapidly growing into a leading watering-place. The numerous inviting cottages add greatly to its attractions, and the softness of the air makes it probably the safest winter retreat for the invalid to be found in the British Isles. Flowers bloom there all the year round, and it is the especial spot of the Isle of Wight where the consumptive can be benefited during the winter months. This is due to the circumstance that the Undercliff faces the southeast, whose breezes are warm and soothing, and is protected from the raw winds of the north and west by the heights of Boniface Down. By the aid of private charity a noble hospital has been established at Ventnor for the benefit of such invalids as have not the means to resort thither unaided, or to go to the yet more advantageous sanitariums farther south.

During the summer the nearness of the Isle of

Wight to London causes it to be overrun by cockneys enjoying their vacation in this paradise. Those who are annoyed by a crowd when seeking the retirement of nature will therefore find the other seasons more agreeable on the Isle of Wight.

THE BAHAMAS.

But all the world's paradises are not confined to the Eastern Hemisphere. The Pacific as well as the Atlantic, America no less than Europe and Asia, invite the wanderer to enjoy the beauty of scenery or revive his failing energies in their paradises as well. Tahiti, Nukahiva, Mauritius, Jamaica, Cuba—the Queen of the Antilles—over whose cliffs the dense umbrage of palms hangs like plumes, and where the lianas, like serpents, embrace in many folds the lithe stems, are gloriously beautiful ; but too often the deadly miasma lurks in their bowers, or over them sweeps the dread march of the hurricane, or they are of such size as really to be excluded from our list of the world's resorts, not because they lack beauty, but because they are allied to continents, and to describe or thoroughly to see and know them would take years, and a separate volume.

With all the proud opulence of its scenery, Cuba failed to win my affections because the fierce and treacherous character of its people, the depressing influences of slavery, ever attended by the stealthy bloodhound, and the sudden cruelty of the yellow fever seemed to overbalance the quality of the scenery, and I care not to see it again.

Not far north, however, are the Bahamas, which offer many of the attractions and few of the disadvantages of Cuba. New Providence, whose town of Nassau is a well-known sanitarium, is from November until May a most winning spot with a moderate and equable temperature, varying only five or six degrees daily. Coralline like its sisters, it is low, but overgrown with a semi-tropical vegetation that lends an indescribable charm to every view. I never could look on a cluster of cocoa-palms without emotion. The most graceful of trees, lithe and delicate as nymphs, when they sway with gentle cadence in the evening breeze, throwing back their long tufts of pendulous leaves like tresses, they resemble maidens bathing by the shore and drying their hair in the wind. In the cocoa we see embodied the mystic poetry of motion and of form, as in no other object in nature except woman.

The trade-winds blow at Nassau. That is enough: it expresses volumes; it means content with life, health, gladness, and repose. No earthly paradise is perfect without the trade-winds, and with them a desert would be endurable. One

does not go to Nassau to find antiquities or delve
into historic lore ; he goes there to bask in the
smiles of Nature in her most gracious moods.

The history of the island is soon told. Time
was when now and again a pirate held sway there ;
Blackbeard was the most noted of these freebooters. In revolutionary times it was a haunt of
Tories, and Lord Dunmore, Colonial Governor of
Virginia, fled thither, and built himself a house
by the sea, which is still standing in the midst of
a charming grove. During the Confederate war
Nassau became a notorious nest for blockade-run-
ners, and enormous profits were realized for a
time. It must be evident that it is a kindness to
the good people of Nassau not to look too curiously into their records. The antiquities consist
of Fort Fincastle, a gray work on the hill behind
the Royal Victoria Hotel, shaped like a paddle-
box steamboat, and another quaint little fort on a
point at the end of the town.

Wrecking and the sponge-fisheries furnish a
general means of livelihood. The former is on
the decline, owing to the increase of lighthouses
and the watchfulness of insurance companies. The
sponge-fisheries give employment to five hundred sloops and schooners, and are very arduous.
Four species of sponge are found there, of which
the kind called the glove is in demand for surgi-
cal operations. As the waters of the archipelago
are very shallow, and generally with a white bot-

tom of fine sand, the sponges are easily seen, and are torn from the rocks by hooks attached to long poles. Negroes abound ; sunlight agrees with them : they are often seen sleeping bareheaded on the hot side of a rock under the beating rays of the sun, where they fairly seem to sizzle ; they enjoy it. They divide their duties between the mysticism and noisiness of fetichism, voodoo-worship, and boisterous Methodism. *Per contra*, the balls at the Government House are very stiff and stately affairs, and formality and pretension have full sway in the upper classes. Intellectual culture is not a prominent feature of the people of the Bahamas, but they probably have enough for their necessities, and enough is as good as a feast.

There are very few places that afford more attractions for yachting and picnicking. The numerous keys offer charming resorts for out-door parties, and there is good sailing in the lagoons which separate them when it is too rough for outside sailing. I shall not soon forget an exciting day when four trim yachts ran across the bar by the lighthouse, and beat in toward nightfall, and the boat I was sailing succeeded in coming in second, although the smallest of the fleet. Sport there is in abundance : sharks for those who like such savage game, and pigeons at the Lakes of Killarney, the pine-circled pools of New Providence, or at the Green Key.

But there is an isle I love better than Nassau,

sixty miles away on the eastern edge of the Bahama Banks; it is Harbor Island, one of the least visited and choicest spots anywhere to be found. I went in the twenty-ton schooner which carried the royal mails. The craft was to sail at sunset, but a conference which the skipper and the writer of these pages held, whittling over the discussion while sitting on the bulwarks, dangling our feet over the transparent water, resulted in the sensible conclusion that it was on the whole expedient for all concerned that the schooner should defer the hour of departure until midnight. By this arrangement I was able to go to a ball that night, where all the wit and beauty of Nassau were assembled, at the elegant mansion of one of her first citizens. After several merry hours, I tore myself away. "Take another claret-cup before you go," said my genial host. Then, leaving behind the glitter and the music, and the eloquent eyes which added such luster to the scene, I rushed out into the starlight and the breeze, and rapidly sped to the harbor-side, where, with her mainsail set, the little schooner chaffed and fretted to get away, like a pawing steed. As I leaped aboard, the skipper cried, "H'ist the jib!" the foresail and gaff-topsail soon followed, and we dropped over the bar, leaving behind a town steeped in liquid shadows and silence. The flash of the lighthouse glanced across the sails as we rounded to on the starboard tack, and the low full moon

11

faced us with a long wake of silver, and whitened
the rocking schooner as she leaned over to the
mild trade-wind, and, slipping by the cocoa-tufted
keys, danced toward Harbor Island.

The next day we hove to off Spanish Wells,
and made a landing to leave a dozen letters for
that island.   It is a quaint, curious, isolated spot,
and the brown huts, elevated on posts by the edge
of a palm-grove at the water-side, were almost as
striking as the lank and singular appearance of
the women.   I confess that I like simplicity and
all that, but must say I draw the line at limp
calico skirts and barrel-shaped sun-bonnets.   The
thatched schoolhouse carried the mind far away
to the missionary schools of the South Sea Islands.
The schoolmaster seemed like one who had not
tasted water for years.   He was actually thirsting
for intellectual nourishment, and followed us to
the boat with an eagerness that was really pa-
thetic.

The devil has a backbone.   I know this to be
a fact, for I sailed by this spinal object in entering the port of Dunmore Town.   At least there
is a long, crooked reef there, which goes by that
name.   How can I ever describe the gorgeous-
ness of the colors of water and sky on that day?
Everything was vivid and intense.   The shallow-
ness of the water over the white coral bottom
gave the sea the color of the most brilliant polished malachite, except where it flowed over ledges

covered with kelp, when it assumed a reddish tint. In the offing the wind deepened the color of the ocean to a dark, almost inky purple, starred with the flash of white-caps and breakers. The cloudless, overarching heavens were rosy-hued, and the darting sea-birds seemed like bearers of light. Swaying groves of cocoa-palms on Harbor Island added yet another indescribable charm to a scene indelibly impressed on my memory, as we shot under the lee of the molten silver tumbling on the reef, and dropped anchor before Dunmore Town.

Harbor Island is but two miles long—a mere dot on the ocean. On the land side is a small town of two thousand people. Each house has its veranda and cocoanut-tree, and back of the town is a grove of palms, dense almost to blackness. On the sea side is a superb coral beach, pinkish white in color and hard as a floor. There the inhabitants sink their wells : after digging a certain depth, the sea filters through the sand purified of its salt, and the sides of the well are kept from falling in by barrels placed one above the other. If there are any other important features about Harbor Island, I did not notice them ; but yet what a magical isle it is ! I never wearied of lying on the veranda and listening to the perpetual roar of the surf and the sighing of the trade-wind in the tree-tops like the music of summer rain. For two pence the round-faced pick-

aninnies would keep me supplied a whole afternoon with jelly cocoanuts and bananas.   And, as
for the pineapples, there are no pines grown anywhere else more luscious than those that the Har-
bor-Islanders raise on a few acres of a certain
red soil at the northern end of Eleuthera, a mile
opposite from Dunmore Town.   Eaten fully ripe,
they are of a sweetness, an aroma, a nectareous
juiciness, a melting succulence, such as no one has
even dreamed of who has not eaten them on the
spot where they are grown.   A field of pineapples is beautiful in color, when the fruit is
allowed to ripen on the stalks ; yellow, scarlet,
and green are interwoven like embroidered silk
and gold on the maroon color of the ground.   Of
course I went to see Bottom Cove, a vast, natural
limestone arch eighty feet high, on the neighboring island of Eleuthera ; it looks much higher
when one stands at its center, where it is but
four or five feet wide and cracked at that.

I also admired the bronze-stemmed and golden-
crested aloes, decoratively soaring above the flat
reaches of Eleuthera.   But, after all, it was the
long, dreamful hours fanned by the sea-winds at
Dunmore Town that kept me lingering there, and
made it almost impossible to sail away into the
nineteenth century again.   To be sure, one is not
so luxuriously entertained on Harbor Island as in
the elegant hotel at Nassau ; but when one lives
out of doors and on fruits, he cares less for artifi-

cial luxuries ; and, until the summer sets in, a more healthful, soul-invigorating air can scarcely be found than that of Harbor Island.

***

FORT GEORGE ISLAND.

WHY is it that small islands have such a charm above large islands ? Explain it as you will, the fact remains. Perhaps it is because one learns their peculiar characteristics sooner, and thus grows familiar with all their attractions, and does not feel as if, like some characters, there is always about them some inaccessible nook that evades search and baffles our most patient scrutiny. At any rate, my vote is for small islands, not above twenty or thirty miles long at the most, and the smaller the better. Fort George Island would seem to come within that category, for it is only a short five miles between its extreme points. Some pragmatical martinets might claim that, as it is only divided by narrow creeks from several other islands, which are in turn separated from each other by seams of sea-water proportionately no wider than the cracks in a geographical puzzle, and as the mainland of Florida is but a few furlongs away, Fort George can hardly be considered an island. I decline to quibble or discuss the question. The

place is entirely surrounded by water, and for in-
sularity a spoonful of fluid will do as well as an
ocean. And so far as concerns beauty, solitude,
or tranquillity, Fort George might as justly be in
the South Pacific as on the Floridian coast ; for
it is tropical in its attractions, and balmy and
healthful as the fountain of youth.

Nature plays a curious illusion with the fancy
at Fort George. The aspect is tropical, the vegetation in copiousness and color suggests a climate
under the line, while the botany is really that of
the north temperate zone, with a few exceptions.
The dense forests are composed of wonderful
wide-spreading oaks, or tall, slender pines ; but
the grape-vines and funereal Spanish moss cling
to them with such serpentine embrace, or so fes-
toon their far-reaching arms, as to convey the impression of tropical scenery ; while about the roots
the spiky palmetto, called the Spanish bayonet, en-
livens the shadowy underwood with the vividness
of its glinting green. Here and there nature has
also planted clusters of cabbage-palms in such a
judicious and effective manner, that when one
sees a group of them in the foreground, and beyond them the yellow sands and the dark azure
of the ocean lashed by the spring trades and
breaking with a triple ridge of foam on the bar at
the mouth of the St. John's River, you can hardly convince him that he is on the coast of the
United States instead of the Windward Isles or

the Philippines. There are three palms at Point
Isabel, two together and one alone on the edge of
a lagoon haunted by blue cranes, which have an
indescribably delicate and suggestive gracefulness
and beauty.

From Barnegat to Key West there is no land
so lofty on our coast as the central ridge of Fort
George Island ; and yet it is only ninety feet high,
although the compact and velvet-like forest which
covers it makes it look somewhat higher. It is in
color, therefore, as much as in form, that one of
the charms of the isle is found. A certain blue
flower opens abundantly every morning before
sunrise, and closes when the sun is high, which
gives a beautiful effect to the grass, and seems to
moderate the heat by the infusion of cool color
into the warm rays falling aslant on the glistening
herbage. Where the forest retires the savanna
is covered with dense salt grasses and diversified
by lofty shell-mounds, overgrown with vines which
have given the scientists no little trouble, for it is
difficult to account for their origin. The mocking-
bird makes the morning hours at Fort George
melodious when he perches in the magnolias and
rapturously flings his wild improvisations to the
breeze.

There is one settlement on the island, called
Pilot Town. It numbers less than a dozen rustic
cottages, and is just inside of the bar. There the
pilots live who take ships up to Jacksonville.

Their lookout is an old mast with a so-called crow's-nest on the trestle-trees at the top. Besides these houses, there are two good hotels for summer and winter, and several attractive cottages sprinkled at intervals in clearings. Some beautiful drives have also been opened through the woods.

The most important place on Fort George is the Homestead, a rambling mansion with four peaked rooms at the angles, giving it somewhat the appearance of a fort. An arm of the sea, which divides Fort George from the snow-like sand - dunes of Talbot Island, is but a stone's throw from the house, and superbly venerable oak-trees bearded with gray moss shade the ground.

Here of old lived and reigned Captain Kingsley, a singular Scotchman who owned the island, and here built the ships which he sent to Africa for negroes to cultivate his cotton. On one of these trading voyages he received from an African prince the present of one of his daughters ; he brought her to Fort George, gave her a smattering of an education, then made her his mistress, and finally married her, and bequeathed plantations to her children. The negro quarters of the old plantation are still standing, in a semi-circle green with ivy around the graves where they were buried, and flanked by a procession of palms. But the slaves are gone, and their tyrant has gone, leaving behind him a name that will live in that region for ages. He was undoubtedly a man of striking and original character, whose bad traits were tempered by many streaks of goodness.

Other scenes this isle has beheld ; for, small as it is, it has yet earned for itself a place on the pages of history. There is no more romantic and thrilling episode in the annals of America than the feud of the French and Spanish adventurers who first colonized the banks of the River of May or St. John's, and built forts on each side of the entrance, where Mayport and Pilot Town now stand, besides a larger fortification six miles up the river called Fort Charlotte.

Of the treachery and fanaticism of Menendez, the surprises, the sieges, the patient endurance, the heroism, and the massacres which attended a bloody struggle that terminated by the successful expedition called the Vengeance of Dominique de Gourgues, one can read with profit and pleasure in Parkman's masterly narrative. But there is one point he fails to make clear, for the reason, if I may venture to say so, that the able historian of those events does not seem to have visited Fort George Island. Why that name should have been given to it has up to this time been a matter of conjecture ; but it seems to me circumstantially evident that it is a corruption of Gourgues, and was taken from the adventurer who, so far as I can judge from a careful consideration of the

scene and subject, captured a Spanish fort on
this very island at the spot alluded to above.
Exactly where stood the first of the three forts
overpowered by the attack of De Gourgues, Parkman does not state. I am quite sure that it was
on Fort George Island, about midway between
Pilot Town and the Homestead.

There, on that memorable day three centuries
ago, the Spanish garrison were taking their dinner
unaware of peril at hand, not even imagining a
French force to be within thousands of miles.
Swimming across the lagoon holding their swords
and tomahawks between their teeth, the French
and their Indian allies, led by Dominique de
Gourgues, burning with fury to avenge his slaugh-
tered countrymen, stole through the forest and
began to swarm over the ramparts. "To arms !
the foe, the foe !" yelled the thunderstruck Spaniards ; but too late. They were taken so unawares that the French swept all before them,
and in a few short moments the whole of the garrison lay dead in that earthwork of the isle hence-
forth to be called Fort George Island.

LAKE GEORGE.

A sail of two hours in a steamer over the
placid surface of the St. John's River took me to
Jacksonville ; thence I flew by rail to the North-

ern States, and found it a not unpleasing transition to pass from the palm-groves of Fort George Island to the lovely bays and romantic cliffs and valleys of Lake George. There are few countries equal in beauty to some of our Northern States; there are few lovelier spots than the valley of Wyoming or the valley of the Housatonic and the Berkshire Hills, or the noble shores of the Hudson. If we could say as much for the climate, who would not be altogether satisfied with the scenery of our country? But the sudden extremes of heat and cold, while they may subserve some wise purpose in strengthening the thews and sinews and brains of the race that is being welded out of many on our shores, do certainly subtract much from the enjoyment of life.

But, taking things as we find them, there is no fairer spot on the continent of North America than Lake George; and it may be added that the climate of the adjacent parts, owing to its elevated position, is during the summer rather more bracing and equable than is generally found in the United States.

Another attraction which the lake possesses above many parts of the country is its treasure of historic associations, in which it resembles some of the most interesting resorts of the Old World. These memories, alternately tragical or glorious, lend a humanizing sentiment to the landscape, and throw around it an aureole which distinguishes and ennobles it above every other lake on the continent.

When the sun drops behind the western range of hills back of Caldwell, and the quietude of evening folds the land in repose, how interesting then to muse on the ruined, moss-green ramparts of Fort George, now hidden in the woods, and musical with song of birds, and recall the day, one hundred and thirty years ago, when the tide of battle surged back and forth around the head of the lake, when Williams and Dieskau fell!—or when we repair to the edge of the lake, where the outlines of the works of Fort William Henry still remain, while the music of the midnight ball floats by, and the distant summer lightning plays over the dark water, the fancy flies back to the siege where French and English and Mohawk met, the three races symbolizing the three great types of modern times, the Saxon, the Latin, and the barbarian, striving for the mastery. The latter won for the time, when the dying shrieks of thirteen hundred murdered Englishmen rang on the air, and testified by their blood the treachery of the French and the cruelty of the Indian. But that tragedy sealed the doom of the dominion of both in America.

A few seasons later, what a magnificent array was gathered at the same spot by Lord Abercrombie—fifteen thousand men in hundreds of boats, with music and banners, gliding down the lake, threading its hundred isles, and bivouacking for the night at Sabbath-Day Point ; then springing up with the morning star at the blast of the reveille, and marching to find their graves around the forest-hidden intrenchments of Ticonderoga ! For a force of that size to embark and to row from Sabbath-Day Point to the end of the lake, then to disembark, to form, and to march to the enemy's works several miles beyond, has always seemed to me a severe day's labor, and to storm the enemy's batteries the same day was too arduous an undertaking, and perhaps contributed to the disastrous repulse of the British.

But defeat with the English generally means ultimate victory, for they nerve themselves to greater energies for the next onset. The following year Lord Amherst accomplished the task in which Abercrombie had failed. Ticonderoga fell, and we all know what soon followed—the capture of Quebec, the death of Wolfe and Montcalm, and the overthrow of the French power in America. Of the numerous legends and events which accompanied or grew out of these stirring scenes, the heroes and the romantic incidents, whose memory clings ivy-like to almost every part of Lake George, one can not talk without writing a volume. But whether one is riding, or sailing, or conversing, they are ever present as an *arrière pensée.*

One of the most interesting objects on the

lake is the grand precipice called the Deer's Leap.
We know not exactly the story which gave a
name to the cliff ; but we readily picture to ourselves an Indian hunter, weary and hungry, who
all a winter's day has vainly sought for game to
carry home to his children in his wigwam.   At
length he starts a roe : she flies before him ; his
arrow wounds but does not wholly disable her.
Despair urges pursuer and pursued.   Suddenly,
as she runs her mad career, staining the snow with
her life-blood, she comes upon the edge of a precipice, but can not turn, for death is at her heels.
With one piteous look behind, she gathers up her
graceful limbs, darts into the air, and, spinning
down the dizzy plunge, falls dead on the rocks far
below.   And so they called that precipice the
Deer's Leap.   How many that we know, hunted
to the death by remorseless destiny, take such a
fatal leap !

But pleasant thoughts are the rule at the lake,
for everything about the scenery is of a character to soothe and fascinate the dreamer who seeks
for rest on its magical shores.

Regarded statistically, Lake George is thirty-
four miles long, and is properly divisible into
three nearly equal parts, each having a distinct
character of its own.   The first division, proceed-
ing northward from Caldwell, extends to Tongue
Mountain and Ten-Mile Island, and is quite broad
at that point.   From Ten-Mile Island is another

division extending to Sabbath-Day Point, narrow and thickly strewed with the Harbor Islands, the scene of a bloody tragedy in the French and Indian wars, and of many a merry "camping-out" party since then. This is the most mountainous part of the lake. On the west side are Tongue Mountain, including the Deer's Leap and Twin Mountain, a lofty, well-wooded ridge, crested by several peaks, and forming the east side of Ganouskie or Northwest Bay, which is the least interesting part of Lake George, although there is a certain grand simplicity about its five miles of solitude and semicircular sweep of hills. Catamount Mountain, a lofty eminence in the northwest, sweeps up from the water with majestic repose.

Opposite Tongue Mountain is Black Mountain, which is a magnificent height soaring twenty-two hundred feet toward the clouds. From certain points it takes the form of a couchant lion, and its somewhat isolated position, as well as the place it holds about midway down the lake, gives it a commanding aspect that adds character to almost every prospect on Lake George. In parts its lines are broken by picturesque ledges or pinnacled rocks that add greatly to its effect.

Bolton Bay and village, including the quaint settlement called the Huddle, at the entrance to Northwest Bay, is one of the choicest spots on the lake, both for the variety and beauty of its views ; and the green islets reposing near it add greatly to the poetry of the locality. No part of the lake is more varied, or as a residence more interesting, affording as it does rare facilities for rowing, riding, and walking. From Bolton we look across by Dome Island into Sheldon Bay, which is overtopped by Pilot, Buck, and Erebus Mountains.

The Huddle, which we can reach either by floating idly over the calm water to Basin Bay, or by an enchanting stroll through the woods, is a settlement that seems asleep under the influence of morphine. A matter of a dozen unpainted, rusty wooden houses, a grist-mill, a post-office, two stores, and a smithy, are grouped on each side of a dashing brook foaming down a steep hillside. Why it should be called the Huddle is perhaps not a question of pressing importance. The woodland nooks in this vicinity are at once picturesque and idyllic.

Gliding across from Bolton, past Green Island, Tongue Mountain, and Fourteen-Mile Island, we come to Shelving Rock, a bold, precipitous slope, said to be infested with rattlesnakes, and adorned by a cascade. Several hotels are happily situated here, commanding at once a view of the broad southern division of Lake George just described, and overlooking the contracted second part of the lake, on which we enter after passing a barrier of islets which shut us in as with a hedge, and give to this portion of the lake an isolated aspect, as if it were a lake entirely by itself. Shut in at either end by islands, and narrowed to a moderate width by the approaching heights of Black and Tongue Mountains, the latter including the Twin Mountain and Deer's Leap, this is the most secluded division of the lake, and reminds one of the narrows of the Hudson. The lake is dotted here with the closely grouped and interlocked islets called the Harbor Islands.

Near the foot of Black Mountain nestles Paradise Bay, so completely hidden by overhanging woods that many would never suspect what beauty lies concealed there unless their attention were called to it. This is quite the loveliest spot in the whole of Lake George. Gliding under the overarching festoons of maple, birch, and pine foliage, we enter into a crystalline basin, glassy and tranquil as if never a breeze ruffled the surface, which is variegated like polished malachite with the wavy reflections of the green woods and islets. We float about the labyrinth of green, and of intermingled shimmering light, shade, and color, as in a dream, so fairy-like and indefinite does it all seem ; for a small peninsula juts out in the center, so indented with scalloped coves as to confuse the outline, while minute tree-tufted islets are so interlocked that it is difficult to discover where one ends and the other begins. Such is the primitive quietude of this magical scene that the water-fowl

12

floating on the surface show no signs of alarm as our boat approaches, but only look at us with surprise that any one should intrude upon their green domain.   Such is Paradise Bay.

Stealing away with regret from this enchanting retreat, we thread the Harbor Islands, which were the scene of a terrible massacre in the colonial wars.   On the 25th of July, 1757, Colonel Parker, with a detachment of four hundred men, bivouacked for the night on these islands, supposing that amid their tangled, wooded mazes they would escape the eagle eyes of the Indian scouts. But he was fatally mistaken.   Stealthy and indefatigable, the Mohawks had tracked the English, and fell upon them unawares in the gray of morning with that whoop piercing the still air which has sent despair to so many hearts.   Out of the four hundred English only twelve escaped.

Having made the ascent of the commanding dome of Black Mountain, which is easily reached from this point by a road opened by Cyrus Butler, Esq., we now approach Hulett's Landing, which is one of the prettiest spots on the lake. A number of ornate cottages, kiosks, and rustic bridges add to the attractions of this place.

Sabbath-Day Point, opposite Hulett's Landing, marks the beginning of the third and last division of Lake George.   Here the lake widens again, and the views from this point are of the most opposite character, and for poetic sentiment and artistic beauty are scarcely equaled by any other landscapes on the western side of the Atlantic.

Looking south, we gaze down the narrows; groups of islets tuft the water; on the right the bold crags of the Twin Mountain are robed in green, over which flow the deep shadows of sunset embroidered with the golden rays that steal through clefts in the ridge. On the opposite side Black Mountain soars with grand reserve toward the zenith, with a matchless majesty of outline, wrapping its slopes in a mantle of purple and flashing back the glory of evening from its thunderous brow, above which the eagle soars alone, like the spirit of an Indian chieftain.

But when we turn and gaze northward, the scene is changed. No islands stud the broad, unbroken expanse, which stretches away before us miles and miles, and so ethereally blue that the heart throbs with joy to behold it. The fading horizon is inclosed with roseate elusive cliffs dipping so magically to meet the water that they seem to lose themselves in a delicate mirage. Here and there a snowy speck of a sail gleams like a star dropped from the sky.

As we approach these highlands they resolve themselves into two headlands, of which the one on the right is Anthony's Nose, at whose base one may look many fathoms down into the clear, sea-green flood. Opposite to Anthony's Nose rises Rogers's Rock, over six hundred feet high, iron-red,

deeply grooved, and precipitous, and reminding
us of an incident of the colonial wars, when the
Indians pursued that gallant border soldier, Captain Rogers, up to the summit of the cliff. It
was in the winter season. Hurling his knapsack
and gun down the side to the ice below, he re-
versed his feet in the snow-shoes and stole back
the way he came, and reappeared to the Indians,
escaping across the frozen lake. They supposed
he had slid unharmed down the precipice by the
aid of the Great Spirit, and gave up the pursuit.

Echo Bay, a charming wood-sheltered cove, is
at the foot of the rock. From this spot, one of
the most impressive and beautiful on Lake
George, the lake gradually narrows, and finds an
outlet two or three miles beyond, escaping by
rapids so musical that the Indians called it Ticonderoga and the French Carillon. The grass-
grown lines, twice assaulted by the English, are
still distinctly visible in the groves ; and a portion
of the fortress of Ticonderoga, the scene of many
interesting episodes in our colonial and revolutionary wars, yet remains on a commanding
height overlooking Lake Champlain, the most
picturesque ruin in the United States.

I sometimes envy those who have not yet
seen Lake George—to whom it is yet an unre-
vealed rapture. There is a great joy in store for
them ; and if they place themselves in a passive
condition, and allow its various moods and attrac-

tions to influence their souls, they will find that it will grow into their existence and become one of the dreams of a lifetime.

THE BERMUDAS.

AND yet—ah ! there is always a *yet* in this unsatisfied nature of ours—my thoughts fly again to the sea, and my love for the fair things of this world craves once more the flavor and the freedom of the salt waves, and the sight of isles of beauty looming above the ocean, and drawing the heart to them like the magnet of the Arabian tale.

If, after roaming over the United States, we are next to visit islands, it is not inappropriate to go first six hundred and forty miles southwest of New York, to the "still vext Bermoothes." The epithet is a very happy one. Shakespeare, with the inspiration of genius, though he had never seen them, yet properly described them. In a milder form we there find a renewal of the climatic contrasts and extremes of the neighboring continent ; an insular temperament at once fascinating and capricious. We find wind there in abundance, but not tempered by the equable regularity and healthfulness of the trade-winds, but tending rather to storms and sudden squalls. They are never

without a wind of some sort at Bermuda ; but
as it always comes off the sea, it is on the whole
not injurious to invalids, except to those who are
rheumatic or in the later stages of consumption,
to whom it is unsafe because the atmosphere is
saturated with moisture that falls not so much
in rain as by a perpetual dampness which takes
the life even out of brimstone-matches. In summer the heat, without being quite so extreme as
in the United States, is still so continuous and exhausting as sometimes to be weakening to invalids, although agreeable to those in good health.

The vegetation also resembles, on a reduced
scale, that of the adjacent continent. Pines and
cedars are the native woods, and potatoes, onions,
and tomatoes the staple products. And yet,
owing to the mildness of the air, the cocoa-palm,
the India-rubber tree, and other exotics can be
easily made to grow there ; while the arrowroot
of the Bermudas is as good as that of the Sandwich Islands. The oleander grows by the roadside in wonderful profusion ; the pepper-tree and
the scarlet-blooming pomegranate flourish in the
gardens ; the mangrove's tangled roots darken
the coral caves of the island coves ; and the angel-
fish, the silver-green, the parrot-fish, and the blue-
fish are gorgeous with the brilliant crimson and
azure colors of the tropics. The trees are full of
singing birds ; one recognizes at morning and
evening the catbird's rapturous warbling, and is

dazzled by the vivid colors of the cardinal-bird darting in the darkling gloom of the groves.

Yet we are nowhere oppressed with the profuse splendor, the prodigal luxuriance of tropical scenery. Everywhere there is evidence of the strictest economy even on the part of nature, and an harmonious effort, with moderate resources, so to combine all the features of the landscape as to produce the effect of the most admirable art. Without any collusion, man and nature have united to achieve this laudable result, and the consequence is, that I know of no spot on the globe where so much has been made out of so little.

There are not above thirteen thousand acres in the whole group, yet they have been so cut up into hundreds of islets, which are more or less joined by dikes or coral bars gradually uniting many of them, and they are so indented with innumerable coves and bays, that one may ride continuously from St. George to Ireland Island, some sixteen miles, while there are actually three hundred miles of excellent roadways in the Bermudas! They were cut in the coral rock by convicts; otherwise they might never have been made!

Then, again, with consummate artifice, Nature has contrived to throw up a low hill in one spot, or scoop out a valley at the next turn of the road, giving to these low isles the impression of a rolling country of large extent, and sometimes within pistol-shot of the sea one may imagine himself in an inland country.

The coral formation of these islands is another mystifying fact. Why, inquires one, should we find islands still actually growing out of coral almost at our very doors—when, too, the northern cedar crests the hills? We can only say it is a freak of nature, and that no other coral island exists so far north. And nowhere else, in this latitude, except around the Italian shores, do we find such vivid and exquisite blues, greens, and purples in the hues of the sea, although common enough farther south, especially when the adjacent shores are coralline. Thus we discover that the Bermudas present a most rare, capricious, and diverse but delightful combination of attractions to the invalid, the artist, or the naturalist, or your mere idle seeker after pleasure.

It is with a feeling akin to wonder that I look back to Bermudan days, and think how simple may be the elements which make up the sum of human happiness. Often they are wholly negative. Freedom from physical discomfort or pain, or from mental worry, constitutes the most perfect form of happiness in this world. Once we begin to add to it a positive, an active character —once we begin to love, to yearn, to seek after— we taste sorrow and find what a bitter possession life may be.

Hamilton and St. George are the towns of Bermuda. The latter is a sleepy, unattractive place with a garrison and a fort. The former is a charming village, surrounded by delicious rose-covered country-seats, and a semblance of activity about its wharves that seems to suggest thrift. Hamilton is reached by a most intricate channel among the islands, after entering the large bay inside of the vast coral reef that subtends on the north the arc made by the curved line formed by the islands. A curious effect is given to the houses peeping above the shrubbery by the dazzling whiteness of the roofs. It seems that, as there is no water to be obtained by digging wells, the people must depend upon the bounty of Heaven dropping directly from the sky; thus all the rainfall on the roofs, which are covered with flat slabs and white cement, is caught and conducted into cisterns.

There are several places of especial interest in Bermuda; although, for that matter, is it not true that, given a certain type of scenery, one who keeps his eyes open and can perceive the subtile suggestions of quiet effects no less than those that are more obvious and notable, will find something to interest and stimulate the fancy whichever way he turns? One of the spots to which I allude is Harrington Sound, a beautiful sheet of water, whose coral bottom colors it an exquisite pale green. The low, overhanging cliffs are honeycombed with caves, and the Flatts village, near the narrow outlet to the ocean, is a charming retreat on a warm day.

Not far off, in a retired nook on the edge of a mangrove pool, is the house in which Tom Moore lived when he was connected with the Admiralty Court of Bermuda. It is difficult to imagine how this frivolous bard was able to live contentedly in these isolated isles. His element was the fashionable drawing-room of London during the season, and there is no evidence that he wasted much enthusiasm over the Bermudas or its people, for, although as soon as he landed he began to scribble amatory verses under a scraggy calabash-tree which is still standing, and professed to love somebody on the islands very heartily, he on the other hand applied certain descriptive epithets to his neighbors which are not more than half true, and are certainly not complimentary.

Captain John Smith, who was by nature far more of a rover than Moore, spoke of these isles in terms of eulogy so lofty as almost to make one doubt either his judgment or his veracity. The people are agreeable and hospitable, and seem to exert themselves to extract the best results out of narrow circumstances. Having no game to hunt, they organize furious paper-hunts, or steeple-chases after an imaginary trail marked out by bits of paper strewed deviously over road and field, and leading up in the most intricate manner to a general rendezvous, where a dinner is served to the wearied hunters.

Then, too, there is a yacht club patronized by half a score of gentlemen with long titles—really a very enterprising association, whose races are full of fun and excitement. The yachts, built of cedar, of a model and rig peculiar to the Bermudas, are very rakish, saucy-looking craft, and go to windward with remarkable ability. They carry a leg-of-mutton mainsail and a jib, and in the races spread a preposterous amount of canvas.

Those who are interested in naval matters can find a morning pass very pleasantly at the dock-yards and arsenal at Ireland Island. The famous floating-dock which was towed from England is also there, and well worthy a visit, especially if some mighty ironclad is undergoing repairs within its tremendous walls.

But the most beautiful and attractive spot in Bermuda is what is most appropriately called Fairyland. There, among the intricacies of winding coves, a labyrinth of islets are clustered, forming a mimic Venice. The far spreading, densely intertwining roots of the mangrove darken the shores, and, while the waters may be elsewhere disturbed by the winds, there all is quietude and peace. To float through Fairyland in the argent light of the moon, with music and fair company, is to eat the lotus and dream that one is in paradise.

TENERIFFE.

EASTWARD once more we turn the prow, to
search for paradises that are easily accessible to
such as wish to find a respite from the vexation,
or the care, or the bad climate of our country,
and desire a temperature more equable and less
boisterous than that of Bermuda. There is "a
mountain islet pointed and peaked" near the
coast of Africa, in the east Atlantic. It is one
of the Hesperides, one of the Fortunate Isles, and
he who has seen it is fortunate among men. The
islanders of other days, those Guanches who once
dwelt there, but whose bones only remain in the
caves of the island—a noble, simple, manly, heroic, and, alas! an extinct race—called their magnificent island Thener-ifé, the White Mountain;
and so to this day it goes by the name of Teneriffe; for the vast volcano is yet there, with its
hoary peak supporting the stars.

At Bermuda and the Bahamas we found a
coral formation, but Teneriffe is altogether igneous. Its tremendous cliffs and sharply serrated
ridges are warm in tone and savage in form,
wrinkled and scarred by the fury of the fiery
trial that formed them ages ago. The adjacent
isles of the Canaries lie around Teneriffe as if it
were their leader; and westerly of the center
soars the Peak, while the island tapers off at the

east end to the lofty and desolate promontory called Anaga Point. A central range bisects the isle, and the city of Santa Cruz lies at its feet on the southern side, bathed by the foam of the trade-wind. There dwell the garrison and the Governor; there are the hotels; and for seven months, from October to May, the air of the place is like balm, and from the flat house-tops one gazes over the sea, and enjoys the fragrant breeze that waves the plumage of the palms.

Under the silvery haze of the moon the lover thrums his guitar, or breathes the universal language that all understand, to the dark-eyed señorita who leans her round arm on her window-sill, and half arrests the fluttering of her fan to catch the utterances of his burning heart. The perfume of the jasmine and the rose steals by like the breath of an unseen spirit; and as the night wears on the *sereno*—so they call the night watchman— takes up the cry, and in long, musical notes soothes you to slumber with the assurance that all is well.

At morning, in answer to the tinkle of the bell, a waiter brings to your bedside spiced choco- late in a silver cup. Then you rise, and, leaning against the railing under the awning that shades your balcony, you may, if so minded, and are not undevotional in your aspirations, look on the tall, slender señoras passing by to mass at the cathe- dral, the lace mantilla thrown over their black

tresses and gracefully drooping over the exquisite shoulders. But this is a dangerous indul-
gence to one who is not piously inclined.

The ways of love are thorny in Teneriffe—so
difficult, indeed, that one may well wonder how
any one can ever be married there. Every one is
a self-constituted spy, and every woman who is
not old and ugly as Hecate is watched as if she
wished to run away with somebody, as I doubt
not many of them would like to do just because
of the perverseness which makes restraint galling
and intolerable. I remember a lithe, graceful,
handsome young girl of sixteen, and of wealthy
parentage, who was staying at the hotel ; she
never stepped foot outside of her room, even for
the mere purpose of promenading in the veranda,
but what she was followed like a shadow by her
grandmother or her mother, or even her father.
And, if she had dared to walk forth alone into the
street, she would have been accosted and insulted
by some rascal in fine clothes ; for it is assumed
in Spanish lands that only an immodest woman
walks the streets alone. Incredible as it may
seem, even the courtesans do not go out unless
accompanied by some old crone ! The glorious
freedom and independence of women in our country is little understood in the Latin lands, where
woman is always treated as if she had no innate
sense of virtue to protect her from the snares of
society.

In Teneriffe a gentleman may not converse alone with a lady unless he is her brother, son, father, or husband, except when they are separated by a wall, she on one side of a window, and he of course on the other side in the street! I never could by any means learn that the people are a whit more virtuous, for all this jealous care, than in lands where more liberty is allowed; in fact, I think they are rather less pure. Offers of marriage are made invariably through the intervention of third parties, unless perhaps when the ladies walk on the plaza in the evening, if opportunity should offer. On such occasions, if a gentleman has a sister or a cousin who feels kindly toward his suit, she may contrive to have his lady-love walk at her side, and thus, while he is ostensibly escorting his sister, he may seize a golden moment to utter his love. A gentleman moving in the best society told me that he had been waiting for such an opportunity over six months, and still had it to hope for.

But there are other places and scenes in Teneriffe, besides the piquant little city of Santa Cruz, that are well qualified to attract the visitor to that island. Indeed, if one finds Santa Cruz charming, what will he say when he comes to Laguna, Icod, and, especially, Orotava—a name I can never pronounce without a thrill of rapture?

I started for the valley of Orotava in a carriage, and followed a fine, broad, zigzag-road up the

mountain-side until we came to Laguna. Soporific
is a mild word to apply to this town ; the very
houses are steeped in slumber, the grass grows in
the streets, the houseleek clambers over the roofs
and casements, and the armorial bearings are
crumbling over many a stately gateway of noble
families gone to decay. Here and there an old ser-
vitor, or a wrinkled priest in black cassock, or an
indolent camel wandering with leisurely and noiseless pace through the streets, indicates that there
is still the breath of life in the musty dwellings of
the old-time capital of Teneriffe.

Thence we passed to the thatched peasant-huts
of Matanzas, which derives its name from the signal defeat that Alonzo de Lugo encountered at the
hands of the primitive inhabitants, the Guanches.
At a time when the Spaniards were trying to gain
a foothold on the island, the Guanches, simple
pastoral people as they were, were yet able to
slaughter six hundred out of the thousand Spaniards they attacked on that day, and the following day slew three hundred more. But the old
story of civilization and barbarism was repeated
here. Bringing reënforcements to their aid, the
invaders ultimately subjugated and exterminated
the brave Guanches.

A curious people were these primitive islanders, whose life and code reminded one of the old
legends about the golden age. Divided into six
tribes, to whose origin we have no clew, they dwelt

harmoniously within the narrow bounds that the ocean had set for them. They had no boats nor ships ; they knew not nor cared not for other lands ; their possessions consisted of flocks, and they lived on milk and corn. Crime was never punished with death ; indeed, innocence seems to have been a characteristic of their simple life. The severest penalty known among them was to degrade those who belonged to a class of chiefs to that of the peasantry. They dwelt largely in the numerous caves of the cliffs formed by the cooling of the lava. The absolute perfection of the climate deprived these caverns of humidity ; and as a chief sat at the entrance of his rock-dwelling at the evening hour, surrounded by his children and attendants, he looked forth on one of the most magnificent prospects on the globe. When they died, the Guanches were embalmed and laid in caves which looked over the surf that beat far below. Sometimes the mummies were lowered by ropes from the top of the precipice ; sometimes, through long, winding, and dark subterranean passages, they were carried by the light of glimmering torches to their last abode. At Icod I followed the windings of such a cave for a third of a mile, often stooping low, until I came to a cavern-hall directly over the ocean ; and there, on ledges around this natural mausoleum, I saw the bones of the Guanches.

But when I came to a place in the road where

13

the valley of Orotava lay spread before me, it
marked an era of my life.   For years I had been
fired by the glowing description of Humboldt,
who declared that in his travels he had seen no
landscape which combined to such a degree the
sublime and the beautiful.   For years I had longed
to visit this enchanted spot, and an imaginary
picture of it was ever floating before my eyes.
It was, therefore, not without emotion that I now
looked upon it for the first time.   That I failed
wholly to appreciate it at once was owing to this
circumstance, and not to any defect in the prospect before me.   Like all other objects of the
highest order of excellence, the full glory of this
valley was not revealed at a glance.   A long acquaintance with it, a familiarity with its various
aspects, is essential before one can fully appreciate
the vastness of its attractions.   In the presence of
a great work of nature or of art, one needs to grow
up to the measure of its grandeur.

The valley of Orotava is not so much a valley
as a slope descending by easy gradation to the
sea.   It is inclosed on three sides by mountain-
ridges and cloven in the center by a ravine.   Its
upper heights are clothed with chestnut-forests,
and it wears on its bosom that quaint and lovely
city of Orotava, where on festal days the ladies
spread the streets with carpets of flowers in elaborate and beautiful patterns, where the surf and
trade-winds beat evermore on the slag of the shore,

where the ships ride exposed to the full brunt of the ocean and fear no gales. There cluster the old convents and Oriental-like mansions of the gentry.

Beyond this town, westward, is the romantic village of Realejo, whose church has a cedar ceiling, which is a very delicate piece of carving. Above the valley of Orotava soars the famed Peak of Teneriffe to the height of nearly thirteen thousand feet. Every feature of this landscape is on a grand scale, all the lines harmoniously converging to produce completeness of effect. Everything seems simple enough at first, but the majesty of the scene increases with every day that one renews his observation.

I ascended the Peak. Everybody who goes to Teneriffe is expected to go up the Peak, but very few do, and I was the first who attempted it that season. The mules of Teneriffe have a very bad reputation, and it is certain that the animal that carried me up to within two thousand feet of the summit was by far the most evil-minded mule on the island. He seemed to kick twice for every step he took in advance; and that my neck was not broken when we descended some of the tremendous precipices of Tigayga, one of the main buttresses of the mountain, will always remain to me an unsolved mystery.

Nearly eight thousand feet above the sea is a crater thirty miles in circumference, whose purple cliffs are two thousand feet high. Across the glaring pumice-stone that forms the floor of the crater we staggered under the terrific heat of the sun to the great lava-ribbed dome which soars four thousand feet higher. Fifteen hundred feet from the summit we spent the night on a two-acre plateau. The surliness of the guides was of a peculiarly exasperating character ; and the fury of the wind, that rose after the gigantic shadow of the mountain on the sea was lost in the shades of night, was of the most boisterous and uncompromising character. The sense of isolation and solitude, with no sign of life apparent but the twinkle of the cold stars overhead, was something that weighed on the soul like a great and nameless presentiment. Stumbling by the light of a dim lantern, at three in the morning, over the rugged, hummock-like piles of lava-blocks called the Malpays, we came at dawn to the second crater, and began the ascent of the Piton. It is a pyramid of pumice-stone over six hundred feet high, terminating in a crater about seventy yards in diameter. The fumes of sulphur which issued from the fissures almost suffocated me. The stones around the rim of the crater, which were yellow with the flowers of sulphur, were hot to the touch. It is useless to describe the sublimity of a prospect that includes within its scope a circumference of over nine hundred miles of the earth's surface, or the imposing beauty of the island be-

low, canopied by the perpetual strata of the trade-
wind clouds. It is one of those scenes that im-
press themselves on the memory for ever, while to
describe it to one who has never seen it, with any
hope of conveying a clear conception of it, is impossible.

The last time I saw the Peak of Teneriffe, the
sun was declining in the west. Slowly the shadows crept up the mighty slopes of Orotava. A
robe of purple mantled the Peak, and above
gleamed its snowy point like a star in the firma-
ment. The hollow chant of the sea floated by on
the evening air. An old man of eighty sat on
the beach, and held in his withered arms an infant
of a day; and I thought to myself: Ages after
they are both gone, the wreaths of vapor will still
ascend from yonder peak; and yet one can say:
"What is man, that Thou art mindful of him, or
the son of man, that Thou visitest him? Thou
hast made him a little lower than the angels, and
hast crowned him with glory and honor."

But one can not always dwell on the heights of
exaltation, and, when the imagination wearies of
the grander aspects of nature, what an infinite
charm there is in its minor details of climate or
vegetation! The fragrance of the fig-trees of
Orotava seemed to make the air heavy; and the
delicious warbling of the capirote, nestling at noonday in the dark shade of the broad leaves, was
wonderfully sweet and inspiring. As for the

climate, it is of a nature to make the simple matter of existence a luxury. For six weeks I saw
the glass vary only four degrees day or night,
while the atmosphere is of exactly that just me-
dium between dryness and humidity which is
fitted to those afflicted with pulmonary or neuralgic and rheumatic complaints. The steadiness
of the trade-winds gives a permanence to the
weather in summer as well as in winter; and the
climate of the valley of Orotava is justly considered by scientists to be the finest in the world.

MADEIRA.

AFTER the valley of Orotava, can there be
scenery to compare with it, or to attract one like
that? I think it is quite likely that there is no
other single landscape equal to that happy valley;
but there is an island three hundred miles away
that, as a whole, is the peer of Teneriffe, offering
within a smaller compass a larger variety of scenery, and possessing a climate that is scarcely
less lovely and healthful. I refer to the island
of Madeira.

I well remember my first arrival at Funchal,
the capital. A great headland had concealed the
city from our view until after nightfall. As the
ship entered the port, nothing was visible but the

dark, vague mass of the island heaving up against the sky. The position of the town was suggested by the rows of street-lights straggling up the mountain-side. The deep shadow of the island was like the gloom of a darker night thrown across the water, over whose tranquil surface floated the strains of music. All was indefinite and mysterious, and of a nature to whet the curiosity and stimulate the imagination. Gradually the music died away, one by one the lights of the city were extinguished, and all was silence and gloom, broken only by the dull, everlasting undertone of the surf, and the flash of a meteor darting at intervals across the zenith, and, with a reflection, rending the tranquil surface of the sea with a quivering line of fire.

I sat up all night, and as dawn deepened into day the island and city were gradually revealed, like a truth long sought that becomes clear when the light of experience enables us to perceive the relations of things ; and the jangle of the cathedral-bells stole across the sea like a welcome to the fairest paradise that man has seen since our first ancestors went forth from Eden.

When Queen Isabella asked Columbus to describe Jamaica, he took a piece of paper and crushed it to a thousand wrinkles in his hand. But if such was a fair description of the topography of that noble island, how much more does it apply to Madeira, which, within the space of

thirty miles in length by nine in width, has along
its coast precipices over which the cataract pours
its silver thread more than two thousand vertical
feet before it mingles with the ocean below ;
while in the center, sculptured into many-colored
Titanic bastions and towers, the mountains rise
abruptly over six thousand feet, and the peaks
are cloven apart by gorges four thousand feet in
depth ! The island is one stupendous corruga-
tion, but between its numberless peaks and ravines includes plateaus and valleys, forests and
meadow-lands, gardens of matchless splendor,
vineyards, and streams. Grandeur and loveliness
here go hand in hand, and the lavish profusion
of flowers beggars all description. I have seen
the roadside for miles on either hand hedged in
by wild fuchsias or geraniums. Where I lived,
the terrace-wall to a height of nearly fifteen feet
was completely hidden by a mass of white and
red double geraniums, growing as vines, and
mingling in their exuberant abundance like a
white and scarlet fire. The roads are sometimes
actually over-canopied by the pink brachts of the
bougainvillia. The strawberries are ripe from
March until September ; the banner-like stalks of
the banana are freighted with fruit for half the
year ; the nectarine and the fig seem always ready
to be plucked ; and the chestnut-forests are weight-
ed with verdure from January to December.

Nor, with all this perennial profusion of na-

ture, and this blending of the plants of two zones,
is the heat of the climate excessive. It has an
equability resembling the serene and sublime rest-
fulness of the Buddhist's Nirvana. On the magnificent plateau of Santa Anna, one thousand feet
above the sea, the mercury for forty years fell
not below 60° nor rose above 80° of Fahren-
heit ; while the dryness and humidity of the atmosphere are so justly proportioned as to produce no sensation of excess in either case. In
the city of Funchal, during the summer, the heat
reaches 85° ; but one can reduce it at any time
by going up to the villas a few hundred feet up
the mountain-sides ; while at the village of Camacha, some three thousand feet above the sea, a
genial average of 65° may be enjoyed for six
months, surrounded by forest, ravine, and stream,
and gazing on the sapphire expanse of the ocean
spreading and vanishing toward the south pole.

The northeast trades blow with unfailing regularity at Madeira, being the great equalizer of
the temperature ; but it is singular that, owing
to the height of the island, these winds are little
felt on the south side, where every morning a
light southerly breeze arises, extending not more
than three or four miles from the land. This produces a remarkable effect of clouds, which is
probably not paralleled anywhere else in the
world except at the Isle of Mauritius. It is seen
at the wild pass of the Serra d'Agoa, beyond the

tremendous abyss of the Grand Corral, where one
gazes on scenes of sublimity rivaling those of the
Yosemite. The hour when the spectacle can be
observed to most advantage is toward evening,
when the sun is low. Blown by the trade-winds
against the mountain-sides, the clouds in vast,
rolling billows are dashed against the crags;
seeking for a vent, like the undertow of surf,
they shoot upward with great velocity, until they
are smitten by the red rays of the sun and look
like masses of flames. But when they reach that
height they strike against the counter-current of
the southerly breeze, which in turn dashes them
back against the fury of the trade-winds. Between the two aërial forces the clouds are driven
upward with lightning velocity, and are instan-
taneously dissipated in the dark blue of the
zenith. Thus, month after month, goes on this
warfare of the clouds, wonderful, terrible, and
glorious, like a vision of the Apocalypse, or like
the pageant of a dream, for without a sound this
pomp and movement of masses passes before the
eyes of the beholder.

Life is what one would suppose amid such
scenery and in such a climate. The labor of ter-
racing, irrigating, and cultivating the steep mountain-sides is enormous, but the simple peasantry
go forth from their thatched flower-tapestried
huts to their daily toil of climbing great heights,
or bearing heavy loads on their heads, with cheer-

ful hearts and songs that, if not strictly musical,
indicate that the cares of existence weigh not
heavily upon them. The question of morals is
not oppressively felt—its code is not severe, and
crimes of magnitude are rare. The duties of religion are easily and pleasantly discharged by a
careful observance of the festivities of holy days.
The dance and the guitar are scarcely less influential than the mass and the vespers, and the ghostly
guides of the people err not by overmuch auster-
ity. One of the most skillful croquet-players it
has been my fortune to encounter was a handsome
young priest of one of the country parishes, who
handled a mallet with as much zeal as if he were
converting the world.

The gentry have a pleasant custom of cele-
brating their birthdays with showers of rockets,
and every parish church has also the annual *fête*
of its tutelary saint, called a *novana*, because it
lasts nine days. The building is ornamented for
the occasion with bowers, banners, and floral dec-
orations, and rockets are sent up by the score at
all hours. Rocket-firing seems to be the favorite
sport of the easy-going people of Madeira.

Portuguese by descent, these islanders combine the qualities of the Spaniards and the French
—not inferior to either in nerve or intelligence,
but with more amiability and kindliness. Their
hospitality and politeness seem to spring from the
heart, and carry the evidence of sincerity.

I remember one day, when I was crossing the
island in a hammock, ascending the steep road
that led up from the wonderful valley of Porto da
Cruz, reposing at the feet of the great rock of
Penha d'Aguia, we came to a halt at a little
open, where there was a stately grove of stone-
pines murmuring on the brow of the precipice,
and a noble villa perched where the ocean seemed
to beat under it two thousand feet below. The
proprietor was seated in the shade of his piazza,
taking his ease and gazing tranquilly upon the enchanting prospect. But when the panting hammock-bearers stopped to rest, he arose, and, coming toward me, an entire stranger, bade me welcome, and with easy urbanity invited me to enter
his house and take some refreshments. To decline
would have been an insult ; I accepted the invi-
tation in the spirit in which it was given, and in
a few moments we were chatting over a collation
of fruits and confections, and a bottle of Madeira's choicest wine.

To these hammock-bearers of whom I spoke,
I owe many of my pleasantest hours in the island.
Where it was difficult or dangerous to proceed on
horseback, they carried me with safety and comfort;
they endured the most arduous toil with cheerful-
ness, and a simple mirth that almost made one forget what a labor it must be to travel some twenty
miles a day over mountains four thousand feet
high, carrying a heavy weight on their shoulders.

The bawling boatmen, bare to the hips, dragging their boats up the steeply shelving beach, through the surf, I also found an amusing class ; and even more entertaining were the grooms who followed the horses. There are no steeper roads than some of those zigzag mountain-paths of Madeira, often hewn out of the solid rock by blasting, sometimes but five or six feet wide, and without the slightest protection, skirting the sides of tremendous precipices overhanging ocean and ravine, where a misstep would hurl one hundreds of feet through the air. But I never doubted my stout gray steed, even in spots where it was not uncommon for travelers to prefer trusting to their own feet. Mounted on horseback, one seems more fully to realize the grandeur and giddiness of climbing or descending a great height, where the waterfall plunges over the road from vast precipices above, while one divides his attention between the thought of how he should land on the rocky shore or the thatched roof of the hut many hundred feet below, supposing the horse should stumble, and the glamour of the bright eyes that startle him gazing through the trellis of a terrace overlooking the road.

At such times what most astonished me was the vast endurance of Manoel, my attendant. One thousand, two thousand, three, and even four and five thousand feet upward, he followed the horse apparently with less fatigue of lungs

than the animal, actually urging him forward up
the rapid ascent as if we were traveling on level
ground. Down those inclines I sometimes descended by sledge over a smooth pavement. The
car was guided by thongs held by men shod in
felt, who stood on the rear end of the runners.
I have thus traversed a distance of two miles from
the Church of Nostra Senhora del Monte to Funchal, and a descent of twenty-two hundred feet,
in seven minutes.

As one looks back over the days so easily
passed in Madeira, he is at a loss to fix on any
one spot which seemed the most attractive, where
all was so beautiful. When in the valley of São
Vincente, in itself a paradise, musical with streams,
surrounded and shut in from the world by the
walls of bastioned precipices, and opening on the
ocean by a mighty gateway cloven by Nature
through the cliffs, then he thinks such another
landscape, such another happy valley, is not found
otherwhere. At Ponta Delgada the vineyards
and the sea, at Porto da Cruz the stately mountains and the sumptuous dales embraced by the
ocean, content the soul; while a night in the old
convent at Calheta makes one say to himself:
"Why, being here at last, should I roam forth
again and battle with a thankless world? Enough!
to know when one is well off is the sum of happiness."

But perhaps the idyllic valley of Machico won

my allegiance more than these, with its miniature
fishing-port, guarded by mighty cliffs and an old
turreted fort, mounted with old-time guns across
whose antique muzzles the spider hath woven her
web. Gradually the bright-green slope inclosed by
mountains rises gently from the water to a villa
and a dismantled convent in the background picturesquely situated and commanding the landscape. The element of humanity, of tragedy, of
legend, has thrown a peculiar interest over this
vale of Machico. As the story runs (a story
mainly true), this is the place where the first landing was made on this island, at least so far as the
memory of man has recorded.

Flying with Robert Macham, her lover, four
centuries ago, from a husband in Devonshire,
whom she had been forced to marry against her
will, and driven by violent gales for weeks on the
boisterous Atlantic, Anna d'Arfet at last saw the
mountains of an unknown isle loom up before her
wearied eyes. At Machico, named after her lover,
she stepped foot on shore, but, exhausted by anx-
iety and fatigue, died three days after. Macham
soon followed her, and they were buried side by
side in this valley. A small chapel which still
stands near the water, surrounded by a pretty
hamlet, is said to be built over their grave.

A tragedy not unlike this, but even wilder and
sadder, happened in Madeira not so many years
ago, which made a yet deeper impression upon me,

because life there is so generally even and uneventful. The gentleman who had purchased the
mansion of the lady of the story, invited me to
dine at his house. In her day of prosperity, seated under the choice exotics of the terraces, she
too had enjoyed the view spread before us, and
sat at the same table where we sat, while my host
repeated to me the romance of her life.

She was married to a husband many years her
senior, who had, however, won the respect if not
the affection of his wife, and they had one child,
a daughter. About that time there came to the
island a Brazilian frigate ; the officers were received with the greatest hospitality by the good
people of Funchal, and balls and *fêtes* followed in
rapid succession.

The commander of the frigate was a Frenchman, who, for political reasons, had been obliged
to fly his country. He was a man of fascinating
manners, great personal attractions, and a magnet-
ism that made him highly dangerous to the sex.
How many hearts he broke while the frigate was
lying in the roads of Funchal the record saith
not. But one conquest he made that boded no
good. The lady of whom I speak met him at a
ball. The lights, the music, the brilliance of his
uniform, the glamour of his station, the subtile
power of his conversation, told with fatal effect on
the infatuated young wife, herself one of the
most lovely and voluptuous beauties in Madeira.

In a few days the frigate was to sail, but ere that hour had arrived the French captain won the lady's consent to leave her child and her home and to fly with him across the sea. The fatal night arrived. Not without a struggle did the victim of a cruel passion forsake for ever the home of her childhood and the infant in the cradle ; but she was driven to her fate by an emotion akin to madness. The frigate's boat was waiting at the beach ; impatiently the captain peered through the darkness for the woman whom he was to steal away to perdition ; the frigate was champing at her anchor, and the land-breeze proclaimed that the hour to sail had come. A dark shadow in a dark night, she came at last, muffled and trembling. Hurriedly the boat was pushed off with its awful freight of despair, and soon shot alongside of the frigate. As the lady and her lover stepped on deck the shrill whistle of the boatswain rang piercingly through the ship, the topsails were sheeted home, and, swinging off from her anchorage like a great ghost against the gloom, the mighty fabric glided away from the island.

The die was cast ; never more could the lady return. The past was irrevocable, and all she now had was the future. The captain led her down the companion-way to the cabin, which she now considered her home ; whatever she had lost for ever, his heart at least was hers, a heart for which

14

she had sacrificed so much. How grateful, how lasting, how entirely her own would be his love! In this mood, and buoyed by the excitement of the hour, the lady reached the cabin, and there a secret was revealed to her with the vividness of an abyss over whose edge one poises, on a dark night, when a flash of lightning bares its appalling depths to the gaze just as he takes the irretrievable step. The lady found herself face to face with the mistress of the fiend who had betrayed her, beautiful and terrible as a tigress, when she also learned that this man had brought a rival on board to supplant her. But one has ever lived who could justly portray the anguish of the scene that followed—the rage, the jealousy, the hate, the remorse, and the despair—he who immortalized the last agony of Othello.

"Let us take our coffee in the garden," said mine host. The coral-tree under which she had sat hung its red bulbs over our heads, like the gems of a fairy bower; but as we gazed on the city below and the conversation took another turn, I still thought to myself, "Will her spirit never come back to haunt her olden bowers and lament over the innocence of her lost childhood?"

And now for Camacha! Manoel led the gray horse to the gate, and we climbed to the village, where I passed my pleasantest days in Madeira. The dew-moistened camellia-trees, drooping with white flowers as if with snow, steeped in the yellow light of the full moon rising above the ocean, the gray mist in the forests and gorges below; the mystery of shadows, the silence of night, the fragrance of gardens, lading the slumberous air with perfume—not once, nor twice, but many times did I gather a rapturous delight from the solemn glory of such nights at Camacha.

But there was one walk at sunset that exceeded all others in this Eden of enchantment. It led to a depression between the hills, which was covered with the dense growth of an ancient chestnut-forest. The superb masses of verdure were beyond compare. Underneath one walked in a cool and emerald gloom, as in a vast temple. Venerable trunks like pillars supported the leafy roof, and in the vista between them the ethereal azure of the ocean was seen, and the roseate mists of evening trailing over it like a procession of naiads. The splendor of the setting sun crept in here and there under the forest, strewing the mossy floor and the stems of the trees with specks of gold, and suffusing the tree-tops with a purple tint like the atmosphere of love. Primeval quietude and peace reigned throughout the serene and majestic glory of the scene. They call this place Valparaiso—the Vale of Paradise.

THE SANDWICH ISLANDS.

It is a long way from the Fortunate Isles of the Atlantic to the Hesperides of the Pacific, but with modern means of locomotion one may soon make the journey. The Sandwich Islands lie twenty degrees north of the line, about 2,000 miles from San Francisco, from which port they may be reached in about eight days, by a steamer which plies monthly to these islands.

The points of resemblance between the Canaries and the Sandwich Islands are quite striking. They are both wholly volcanic in origin; the soil is similar; and the coast-line is often exceedingly abrupt, terminating in tremendous precipices sometimes extending for miles. Both have a climate of extraordinary equability, and are alike fanned by the beneficent airs of the trade winds ; and both, when discovered by Europeans, were inhabited by primitive races, of which one has become extinct and the other has been rapidly approaching the same fate until recently. Each also adopted the religion of the foreigners.

But here the parallel ceases; for, whereas the Guanches became Christians at the point of the sword, the Sandwich Islanders accepted the religion of the Cross voluntarily when borne as a message of good will by missionaries.

Although on the vast expanse of the Pacific

these eleven isles are mere minute specks, yet they contain some 6,000 square miles, an area larger than Connecticut and Rhode Island, Hawaii alone, the largest of the group, being the size of the former State.

Notwithstanding the very considerable extent of the dominions of King Kalakaua, the total population of these islands at the last census was only 57,985. Fifty-five years ago the natives numbered 142,000, and now they are reduced to 44,-000. The remainder are foreigners, chiefly Americans and Chinese, the latter being employed as coolies on the plantations.

Many causes are assigned for the depopulation of these islands; but as this has also been the case elsewhere when the superior has come in contact with the inferior race, we can find no better solution than the Darwinian theory of selection and survival of the fittest. But the extinction of the Hawaiian islanders seems for the present to be checked, and perhaps for a while they may hold their own, until finally absorbed into the white race.

It is exactly one hundred years since Captain Cook was killed in Kealakeakua Bay. The islands had been discovered two centuries earlier by the Spaniards, but it was the death of Cook that brought them suddenly into the prominent position they have ever since held before the world. The French Revolution and the American Civil

War have occurred since then—mighty events in
the history of civilization, whose results shall
"spin for ever down the ringing grooves of"
time.

Less clamorous and attended by no bloodshed
has been the revolution which, during this period,
has transformed the Hawaiian race from a savage
condition to a high rank among civilized states, as
regards education and beneficent government.
King Kamehameha, by his genius and force of
character, unconsciously prepared the way for the
social changes which were to come over the Hawaiian Islands, when he subdued the various chiefs
and islands, and brought them under a common
sway. With the keen vision of a born ruler and
man of destiny, he saw how he might turn to account the appliances of civilized races, and caused
a fleet of small schooners to be built, in which he
was able to carry his army from island to island.

When therefore, fifty-nine years ago, the American missionaries landed on those islands to elevate
them from heathenism and barbarism to Christian-
ity and civilization, they had not to combat separate tribes and independent chieftains, but a nation so united that if an impulse seized one part
the whole would follow. Thirty-three years after
the arrival of the first missionaries at the islands,
the American Board was able to say that "the
Sandwich Islands, having been Christianized, shall
no longer receive aid from the Board."

In that brief period of thirty-three years a people had been transformed from a savage state to a high order of civilization. In that time a written language and a literature were created and education so generally diffused that to-day hardly an adult native can be found who is unable to read and write. A constitutional form of government has been firmly established with a legislative body, and a code prepared by Judge Lee is in active operation; and whereas formerly thieving and murder and obscenity were universal and women were treated as menials, now one may sleep with unlocked doors, and go hither and thither about the islands with a security for life and property equaled in no other part of the globe. Of course I would not affirm that vice does not exist, but it is obliged to keep out of sight, and is as much the exception now as honesty and virtue were before the missionaries arrived.

One of the most characteristic evidences of the transformation which has come over the Hawaiian Islands is shown by the fact that there is a theatre at Honolulu, of which an amusing account is given in the life of Mathews the comedian, who spoke of Honolulu as "one of the loveliest little spots on earth." Mathews acted there "by command of His Majesty Kamehameha V., King of the Sandwich Islands" (not Hoky Poky Wanky Fum, as erroneously reported), and a memorable

night it was. Was it nothing to see a pitfull of
Kanakas, black, brown, and whity-brown (till
lately cannibals), showing their white teeth, grin-
ning and enjoying "Patter and Clatter" as much
as a few years ago they would have enjoyed the
roasting of a missionary or the baking of a
baby ?

In justice to the Kanakas aforesaid, it should
be said that they never in the worst days were
cannibals from choice ; that is, they never ate any
one as a delicacy or even for the more prosaic
matter of nourishment. Only when their chiefs
died, and out of respect or for some religious
notion, they sometimes picked their bones. Although Christianized, it would therefore not be
strange, but rather altogether to be expected, that
the natives should retain some relics of their former superstitions, if not from belief, from habit
and heredity, even after the meaning of the custom is forgotten. And such we find to be the
case in a few instances. Lecky has shown in his
graphic style how religious customs cling to a
tribe or people for thousands of years, sometimes
clothed with new names or adaptations, but yet
originating far back in primordial times.

One of the most interesting signs of the lingering power of old customs is seen in the continued
respect paid to the lineal descendants of the old
chiefs or chiefesses, who, without the slightest authority for doing so under existing circumstances,

sometimes arrogate and are allowed to exercise rights which can never again be legally theirs. The *lomi-lomi* is another habit retained from the past. Those who have been in a Russian bath will have some idea of *lomi-lomi*. It is employed as a means for relieving fatigue, neuralgia, or any physical exhaustion, for assisting digestion, and generally aiding the action of the functions of the body. One lies down, a muscular native with soft hands grasps every muscle in turn, and with a peculiar movement kneads and soothes it, until after half an hour the patient drops off in a sleep more calm and refreshing than that caused by the most beneficial anodynes. In former times the chiefs kept skilled attendants expressly for this service.

The islanders all wear clothes now, but naturally the mildness of the climate makes this somewhat irksome, and men at work often reduce their wardrobe to a minimum consistent with actual decency. The women are clad in a loose dress which is not unpleasing, and at least enables them to preserve the graceful outlines which the fashions of civilization so often deform. They have a pretty custom of adorning their hair with garlands of flowers.

The swimming feats of the Hawaiian islanders have long been famous, not only for sudden exertion, but for long endurance and the power to sustain themselves many hours at the surface ; and women as well as men excel in this useful and noble sport. Infants often learn to swim before they are able to walk.

It is among the rollers at Hilo, on the island of Hawaii, that one sees exhibitions of what is probably the most extraordinary skill ever exercised by man in practicing the powers of flotation. The surf-board play is an ancient custom of the islands, but there is evidence that it is gradually going out of use. The first essential to this sport is a high sea, causing rollers combing over with regularity and height. The second requisite is a bread-fruit-tree plank, ten to twenty feet in length and about two in breadth. Taking this in his hands, the swimmer cleaves his way to the first line of breakers. Then, watching his opportunity, he dives under a coming sea, and is carried by the undertow some distance from the shore, when he rises to the surface and again awaits his opportunity. Soon a breaker of more than usual size heaves up, and as it takes the ground curls upward, and with a speed of forty miles an hour rushes toward the land. At once the swimmer throws himself on his board, and, keeping on the smooth slope of the mighty breaker just under the curling crest, is swept with lightning velocity to the shore. Sometimes some swimmer of unusual hardihood and skill stands upon the surf-board, depending on his balancing powers to escape the fury of the seething surge that ever threatens to swallow him up. The sight is of

the most thrilling character, and one is not surprised to learn that sometimes the daring adventurer loses his life for his audacity. The philosophy of the sport seems to be that it is only possible when the waves roll in obliquely toward the
land. As one part of the comber touches the shore
and breaks and dissolves, the continually repeated action sends the board forward as well as side-
wise ; and thus between forces acting in a tangent
the swimmer is impelled safely where one would
suppose only destruction could be his fate. It is
altogether likely that the discovery of the possibility of thus gliding along the slope of a breaker
was due to accident, like so many other inven-
tions.

Honolulu, the chief town of the Sandwich
Islands, is on the island of Oahu, and if one goes
by steamer it is there that he makes his first landing. It is a most delightful place at the bottom
of a bay, on a plain flanked by hills and dominated
by an extinct volcanic peak called Diamond Head,
soaring near the watering-place Wakiki, and is
embowered amid luxuriant masses of tropic vegetation. The groves of tall, slender palms, gently
swaying in the trade-wind, add an indescribable
charm to a scene that is qualified to intoxicate the
senses with its suggestions of enchanting repose.

But on landing one is struck by the contrast
between the scenery and the architecture of the
city. Every house bears unmistakable evidence

of Yankee origin. The churches, dwellings, and schools are exact copies of such structures in New England, excepting perhaps here and there a veranda that is more in harmony with palm-groves than the white wooden walls and severe lines of American domestic architecture, which is happily giving place to more artistic styles. The society, also, is so largely American or formed on American social models, instead of being of the sensuous, unintellectual, passionate types one meets generally in those latitudes, that it seems as if two effects or scenes were here in conflict and not yet quite adjusted to each other ; while the shipping in the port is so largely of the rig and flag of the United States that the effect is intensified. The American missionaries, not satisfied with imparting their creed into these isles, also grafted American traits into the very character of this insular kingdom, as if anticipating that eventually they might become annexed to the United States.

There is a large, commodious, and excellent hotel at Honolulu, canopied by tropical foliage ; and there also are the palace of the king and other buildings of the government. It sounds strange to speak of these, together with the regularly collected revenues, the well-ordered system of taxation, and all the other adjuncts of advanced civilization, when one considers that not two generations have elapsed since these islands were sunk in primeval barbarism. It is the most extraor-

dinary transformation known in history. Everything, however, is in miniature, except the scenery,
which is everywhere on a grand scale, sublime for
its precipices and gorges, superb for the beauty of
the vegetation and the noble reaches of valley and
plain, ever terminating at the blue expanse of the
ocean, the mighty Pacific, whose rollers playfully
yet majestically encircle the shores, lovingly and
yet exclusively, as if they would shut out the bustle and raging of the busiest century that ever the
sun shone on.

And yet, with all this outward peace, these
islands inclose within the bosom of their stupendous mountains the wildest exhibition of physical
power in action to be seen on the planet. One
would not imagine this from an external or distant view of the volcanoes ; for, unlike Teneriffe
or most other volcanic heights, they ascend by a
very gradual slope, and are dome-like in shape,
without anything striking about them except
their enormous height. Haleakala, on the island
of Maui, is ten thousand feet high, and its crater,
thirty miles in circumference and two thousand
feet deep, is of similar dimensions to the crater of
Teneriffe, but far less regular and impressive. It
has been extinct for untold ages. Mauna Loa, on
Hawaii, has an elevation of fourteen thousand
feet. But the ascent of these heights is everywhere gradual and unattended with danger, until
one reaches the craters. Then, indeed, if they

are in violent action, the adventurer must literally look to his steps.

There are small schooners plying between the islands, and to one who loves the sea it is pleasanter to make the run to Hilo from Honolulu by this means in preference to the small packet steamers. It is from Hilo, on Hawaii, that one can best ascend Kilauea ; and there is a small house at the summit for the accommodation of travelers, where one may be comfortably provided and refreshed, including the ever-grateful application of the *lomi-lomi.*

Hilo is a charming, dreamy little place, straggling along the curve of a fine beach, and nestling picturesquely amid its groves of breadfruit and pandanus trees, above which the delicately limbed, graceful cocoas wave aloft their banners of green, while the northeast trade-wind whispers tender music in the slowly swaying foliage. There is a delightful circle of Americans at this port, who are ever hospitably intent toward the stranger from a foreign shore, who, in the absence of a hotel, must find a shelter under a private roof.

It is here one procures a guide and horses suitable for a trip to the volcanoes. These, according to the old traditions of the islands (not unlike a Greek mythological tale in its character), are under the supervision of the goddess Pele, who superintends the sublime spectacle of fire which renders Kilauea and Mauna Loa the most vivid illustrations of hell which we have at present any opportunity of seeing. Few people care to see more. After a wearisome but very interesting ride over bridle-paths of the roughest character, worn into the lava-beds over which we pass, we arrive at nightfall at the Volcano House, near the edge of the crater of Kilauea, whence after dark the lurid glare of the crater can be seen, and the tongues of flames shooting awfully and mysteriously above a lake of fire. Lying in bed, we see the glare through the window, throwing a glow over the walls. One who is superstitious may well feel awesome at the sight. It must have been some such spectacle that gave rise to the Dantesque visions of the Middle Ages.

Thin clothing is desirable when one enters the crater. It is about nine miles round, and perhaps a thousand feet deep. By steps in the cliff one descends without much difficulty to the dead dry crust which covers much of the bottom of the crater. Near the center is the burning lake of liquid lava, which is rather in the form of two caldrons, but often the lava boils over the barrier that divides them. A natural bulwark rising like a mound around them keeps the liquid fire from running over on the dead but warm lava that forms the floor of the crater. Probably there is no more remarkable and dreadful looking spectacle in the world, or one more suggestive of destruction. The red, fiery, weltering waves boil up and roll over with appalling grandeur, while the heat of the crust, from which we gaze on the scene, is sufficiently warm to make it difficult to stand long in one place.

Mauna Loa, which is much higher than Kilauea, has long been even more celebrated for its fireworks, and within the last generation several violent eruptions have occurred. In 1855 a new crater was formed, which for ten months poured out a stream of burning lava extending seventy miles, and averaging three miles in breadth, and in some places hundreds of feet deep. It rolled over mighty precipices into the sea, a living cataract of fire. In 1859 the same mountain belched forth a torrent of lava fifty miles long in the short space of eight days.

Of course, in a sketch like this, it is impossible to go into an elaborate description of these volcanoes, or of the many phases of scenery which offer themselves in a group like the Hawaiian Islands. Hawaii is corrugated and seamed by numerous cañons or gulches, often of great depth. The *pali* or vertical precipice which forms the northern side of Molokai is also a feature of the island scenery which strikes the beholder with awe and wonder. It resembles the abruptness of Alderney Island, although on a far grander scale.

The islands are often clothed with dense forests, especially on the northern side, which is exposed to the trade-winds, and herds of wild cattle roam at will through the underwood ; while game, such as wild pigs, snipe, plover, and duck, abound. There is, however, much land on most of the islands which is arable, and wheat, maize, tobacco, arrowroot, rice, sugar, and coffee are raised without difficulty. Taro, which is to the Sandwich Islander what rice is to the Chinese or the Bengalee, is raised on low wet ground, which is productive for this root to an extraordinary degree. Horses are so numerous that there is probably more than one for every soul in the islands, although it is not fifty years since they were introduced there. It is often actually cheaper to buy a horse there than to hire one.

Kealakeakua Bay, on the southern side of Hawaii, is the most historical spot in the group. There Captain Cook was killed when attempting to embark, and his bones for years after were worshiped by the natives as those of a god. A village on a little plain at the foot of lofty precipices, flanked by rows of cocoa-trees, by the sea, the place is well worth visiting apart from its tragic associations.

Separated from the rest of the group, Kaui is remarkable as presenting a different formation from its neighbors ; or rather, while of volcanic origin, it shows no signs of igneous activity for many ages past. The rocks and soil, worn down by time, have a more mellow, inviting appearance, and are perhaps better suited to agriculture

15

than the adjacent islands. The Falls of Waia-
lua, rushing over cliffs of basalt, are a beautiful
spectacle ; and the mountains generally, although
lower than on Hawaii, are more stern and massive, deeply furrowed as they are with mighty
grooves and scarped into precipices. The *pali*
of Kaui extends for nearly twenty-five miles
along the coast, resembling the northern side of
Madeira, and only accessible to boats at certain
points in the beach at the foot of the tremendous
precipice. There is something wonderfully grand
in the sublime monotony of such vast insular precipices, lashed for evermore by the surges of the
trade-winds, which tends to increase the sense of
isolation we attach to small islands.

But after we have roamed over the Sandwich
Islands, climbed their mountains, shuddered at
their volcanic terrors, or been entertained by the
curious traits of the native character, it is to the
climate that I revert with the greatest pleasure.
So balmy and regular is it that no word exists in
the Hawaiian language to express weather. Of
course the weather is always good, unvaryingly
good ; therefore it is not weather, for that implies
variability, contrast, and change in atmospheric
conditions. In trade-wind islands you rarely hear
the weather alluded to ; as a stock topic of conversation, which it is in rougher climes, it is sent
to Coventry. When a gentleman calls on a lady,
he must find some other subject with which to

open conversation; for, if he should say, "It is
fine weather to-day," his companion would most
likely stare at him and be inclined to reply,
"Well, what of it? Do we have any other
weather here? Is it not fine every day?"

The northern side of the Hawaiian isles, being
exposed to the trade-winds, which concentrate the
moisture on the mountain-sides, is more rainy than
the lee side; this is especially noticeable on Hawaii. But there is no regular rainy season. The
mean temperature of the islands is about 75°, the
maximum being 90° and the minimum 55°. It
rarely falls to the latter figure at the sea-level;
but by ascending three or four thousand feet one
can find an average temperature ranging from
40° to 75°.

Thus we find a nearly perfect climate here,
slightly warmer than Teneriffe and Madeira, and
somewhat more moist, and therefore, perhaps,
more relaxing, at least to permanent residents who
have no disease. But this objection may apply
to most steady, serene climates, and can be overcome by an occasional absence and bracing up
elsewhere. The invalid who has not yet reached
the point where nothing can ameliorate a permanently disorganized system, is greatly benefited
and often cured by a residence in such a climate,
where he breathes constantly the pure oxygen of
heaven, and seems each day to take a fresh
draught from the fountain of youth.

When I think of life in such a magical spot, when I recall the days and years I have passed in trade-wind islands, I find the utmost degree of enthusiasm reasonable in dreaming of the charms of existence there, and wonder that, having once tasted of what it is to live, one can ever be content to struggle to keep soul and body together in more inhospitable climes. One great blessing of life in such lovely seclusion and climatic independence as that of the Sandwich Islands is, that the problems of life weigh less heavily upon the mind, and one is more content than in the restless society of Europe or America to leave to another world the solution of questions which we can not settle in this; and although that is but a negative advantage as compared with the illusive hopes and stormy raptures which are too often followed by the reaction of crushing despair, content with the present is, after all, the only form of happiness worth the name in this life. The next will reveal whether there is anything better in store for an oppressed humanity; but meantime let us enjoy these earthly paradises which lure us to repose and content, and for a while make us forget.

THE END.

APPLETONS'

New Handy-Volume Series.

*Brilliant Novelettes ; Romance, Adventure, Travel,
Humor ; Historic, Literary, and
Society Monographs.*

---

1. JET: Her Face or her Fortune? By Mrs. ANNIE ED-
   WARDES, author of "Archie Lovell," "Ought We to visit
   Her?" etc. 30 cents.

2. A STRUGGLE. By BARNET PHILLIPS. 25 cents.

3. MISERICORDIA. By ETHEL LYNN LINTON. 20 cents.

4. GORDON BALDWIN, and THE PHILOSOPHER'S PEN-
   DULUM. By RUDOLPH LINDAU. 25 cents.

5. THE FISHERMAN OF AUGE. By KATHARINE S. MAC-
   QUOID. 20 cents.

6. ESSAYS OF ELIA. First Series. By CHARLES LAMB.
   30 cents.

7. THE BIRD OF PASSAGE. By J. SHERIDAN LE FANU,
   author of "Uncle Silas," etc. 25 cents.

8. THE HOUSE OF THE TWO BARBELS. By ANDRÉ
   THEURIET, author of "Gérard's Marriage," "The Godson of
   a Marquis," etc. 20 cents.

9. LIGHTS OF THE OLD ENGLISH STAGE. Biographical and Anecdotical Sketches of Famous Actors of the Old
   English Stage. Reprinted from "Temple Bar." 30 cents.

10. IMPRESSIONS OF AMERICA. From the "Nineteenth Century." By R. W. DALE. I. Society. II. Politics. III. Popular Education. IV. Religion. 30 cents.

11. THE GOLDSMITH'S WIFE. By Madame CHARLES REYBAUD. 25 cents.

12. A SUMMER IDYL. By CHRISTIAN REID, author of "Bonny Kate," "Valerie Alymer," etc. 30 cents.

13. THE ARAB WIFE. A Romance of the Polynesian Seas. 25 cents.

14. MRS. GAINSBOROUGH'S DIAMONDS. By JULIAN HAWTHORNE, author of "Bressant," "Garth," etc. 20 cents.

15. LIQUIDATED, and THE SEER. By RUDOLPH LINDAU, author of "Gordon Baldwin," and "The Philosopher's Pendulum." 25 cents.

16. THE GREAT GERMAN COMPOSERS. By GEORGE T. FERRIS. 30 cents.

17. ANTOINETTE. A Story. By ANDRÉ THEURIET. 20 cts.

18. JOHN-A-DREAMS. A Tale. By JULIAN STURGIS. 30 cts.

19. MRS. JACK. A Story. By FRANCES ELEANOR TROLLOPE. 20 cents.

20. ENGLISH LITERATURE. From 596 to 1832. By T. ARNOLD. Reprinted from the "Encyclopædia Britannica." 25 cents.

21. RAYMONDE. A Tale. By ANDRÉ THEURIET, author of "Gérard's Marriage," etc. 30 cents.

22. BEACONSFIELD. A Sketch of the Literary and Political Career of Benjamin Disraeli, now Earl of Beaconsfield. With Two Portraits. By GEORGE M. TOWLE. 25 cents.

23. THE MULTITUDINOUS SEAS. By S. G. W. BENJAMIN. 25 cents.

24. THE DISTURBING ELEMENT. By CHARLOTTE M. YONGE. 30 cents.

25. FAIRY TALES: Their Origin and Meaning. By JOHN THACKRAY BUNCE. 25 cents.

26. THOMAS CARLYLE. His Life—his Books—his Theories. By ALFRED H. GUERNSEY. 30 cents.

27. A THOROUGH BOHEMIENNE. A Tale. By Madame CHARLES REYBAUD, author of "The Goldsmith's Wife." 30 cents.

28. THE GREAT ITALIAN AND FRENCH COMPOSERS. By GEORGE T. FERRIS. 30 cents.

29. RUSKIN ON PAINTING. With a Biographical Sketch. 30 cents.

30. AN ACCOMPLISHED GENTLEMAN. By JULIAN STURGIS, author of "John-a-Dreams." 30 cents.

31. AN ATTIC PHILOSOPHER IN PARIS; or, A Peep at the World from a Garret. Being the Journal of a Happy Man. From the French of EMILE SOUVESTRE. 30 cents.

32. A ROGUE'S LIFE. From his Birth to his Marriage. By WILKIE COLLINS. 25 cents.

33. GEIER–WALLY. A Tale of the Tyrol. From the German of WILHELMINA VON HILLERN. 30 cents.

34. THE LAST ESSAYS OF ELIA. By CHARLES LAMB. 30 cents.

35. THE YELLOW MASK. By WILKIE COLLINS. 25 cents.

36. A-SADDLE IN THE WILD WEST. A Glimpse of Travel. By WILLIAM H. RIDEING. 25 cents.

37. MONEY. A Tale. From the French of JULES TARDIEU. 25 cents.

Appletons' New Handy-Volume Series is in handsome 18mo volumes, in large type, of a size convenient for the pocket, or suitable for the library-shelf, bound in paper covers. A selection may be had of the volumes bound in cloth, price, 60 cents each.

*** Any volume mailed, post-paid, to any address within the United States or Canada, on receipt of the price.

D. APPLETON & CO., Publishers,

549 & 551 Broadway, New York.

COLLECTION OF FOREIGN AUTHORS.

THE design of the "Collection of Foreign Authors" is to give selections from the better current light literature of France, Germany, and other countries of the European Continent, translated by competent hands. The series is published in uniform 16mo volumes, at a low price, and bound in paper covers and in cloth.

<table>
<tr><td></td><td>PAPER.</td><td>CLOTH</td></tr>
<tr><td>I. SAMUEL BROHL AND COMPANY. A Novel. From the French of VICTOR CHERBULIEZ . .</td><td>$0.60</td><td>$1.00</td></tr>
<tr><td>II. GERARD'S MARRIAGE. A Novel. From the French of ANDRÉ THEURIET . . . .</td><td>.50</td><td>.75</td></tr>
<tr><td>III. SPIRITE. A Fantasy. From the French of THÉOPHILE GAUTIER. . . . .</td><td>.50</td><td>.75</td></tr>
<tr><td>IV. THE TOWER OF PERCEMONT. From the French of GEORGE SAND . . . .</td><td>50</td><td>.75</td></tr>
<tr><td>V. META HOLDENIS. A Novel. From the French of VICTOR CHERBULIEZ. . . . .</td><td>.50</td><td>.75</td></tr>
<tr><td>VI. ROMANCES OF THE EAST. From the French of COMTE DE GOBINEAU . . . .</td><td>.60</td><td>1.00</td></tr>
<tr><td>VII. RENEE AND FRANZ. From the French of GUSTAVE HALLER . . . .</td><td>.50</td><td>.75</td></tr>
<tr><td>III. MADAME GOSSELIN. From the French of LOUIS ULBACH . . . .</td><td>.60</td><td>1.00</td></tr>
<tr><td>IX. THE GODSON OF A MARQUIS. From the French of ANDRÉ THEURIET . . . .</td><td>.50</td><td>.75</td></tr>
<tr><td>X. ARIADNE. From the French of HENRY GRÉVILLE</td><td>.50</td><td>.75</td></tr>
<tr><td>XI. SAFAR-HADGI; OR, RUSS AND TURCOMAN. From the French of PRINCE LUBOMIRSKI</td><td>.60</td><td>1.00</td></tr>
<tr><td>XII. IN PARADISE From the German of PAUL HEYSE. In Two Volumes . . . . . . Per vol.,</td><td>.60</td><td>1.00</td></tr>
<tr><td>III. REMORSE. A Novel. From the French of TH. BENTZON . . . .</td><td>.50</td><td>.75</td></tr>
<tr><td>IV. JEAN TETEROL'S IDEA. A Novel. From the French of VICTOR CHERBULIEZ . . . . .</td><td>.60</td><td>1.00</td></tr>
<tr><td>XV. TALES FROM THE GERMAN OF PAUL HEYSE . . . .</td><td>.60</td><td>1.00</td></tr>
<tr><td>XVI. THE DIARY OF A WOMAN. From the French of OCTAVE FEUILLET . . . .</td><td>.50</td><td>.75</td></tr>
<tr><td>XVII YOUNG MAUGARS. From the French of ANDRÉ THEURIET. . . . .</td><td>.60</td><td>1.00</td></tr>
</table>

D. APPLETON & CO., Publishers, New York.

* Either of the above volumes sent by mail, post-paid, to any address in the United States or Canada upon receipt of the price.

APPLETONS' NEW HANDY-VOLU

[CONTINUED FROM SECOND PAGE OF COVER.]

D. APPLETON & CO. 549 & 551 Broadway